More

Than

Murder

More

Than

Murder

brenda J. woody

authorHOUSE®

AuthorHouse™
1663 Liberty Drive
Bloomington, IN 47403
www.authorhouse.com
Phone: 1-800-839-8640

First published by AuthorHouse 4/15/2009

ISBN: 978-1-4389-5975-7 (sc)
ISBN: 978-1-4389-5976-4 (hc)

Library of Congress Control Number: 2009902842

Printed in the United States of America
Bloomington, Indiana

This book is printed on acid-free paper.

Table of Contents

Preface

This novel is a work of fiction; however, it is based on the true story of an unsolved triple murder that occurred in Western North Carolina during the mid 1960's.

The ill-fated investigation into the murders immediately created suspicion and incensed the imaginations of the community. Rumors of cover-up, conspiracy and bungling still exist after more than forty years. Motives for the murders were as numerous as the list of suspects, yet no one has ever been charged with this horrific crime and all evidence relative to it has disappeared.

This fictional tale focuses on only four aspects of the complex story... all culminating within a few hours on the afternoon of Sunday, July 17, 1966. While elaborating on few of the publicized theories, the author leads the reader along a path of suspicion as she incorporates rumors with less publicized events weaving a gripping tale of sex, drugs, blackmail and conspiracy.

Reference has been made to several local streets and addresses, many of which have been previously publicized and are believed to be correct; however, the characters and events surrounding them are purely fictional.

While delving into the various aspects of this intriguing story, please keep in mind that this is a "*Novel*" and in no way intends to solve this mystery, much less accuse or implicate anyone.

More

Than

Murder

The Beacon Club.....

The morning was already sultry, as the temperature and the humidity were in competition to see which could make humanity the most miserable. Reddick needed to be out at daybreak to have the coffee pot at the Club going before his friends and most trusted associates arrived. The guys hadn't been too happy to hear from him so early in the morning, especially on a Friday.

As he made his way through the empty streets of the small mountain town, he continued to turn the events of the early morning over in his mind. For hours now, that was all he had been able to think about. The reality that his younger brother Bruce had returned to his old habits was disappointing enough, but to learn his depth of involvement in this ongoing 'town scandal' seemed to be too incredible to comprehend. Things had been quiet for so long, Reddick assumed the storm of Bruce's unacceptable behavior had long passed. He even had the Old Man believing Bruce had outgrown the parties and drinking.

It didn't set well with Reddick or his wife Penny when Bruce knocked on their door in the middle of the night in a drunken state. He had put them through this nonsense before and Penny had made it clear she had no intentions of permitting any sort of re-play. He well remembered Bruce's last little episode. Penny took him in and helped him just like he was her own brother. Then, after the dust settled, Bruce seemed to have forgotten how she had befriended him. There wasn't a hint of gratitude from him, not even a simple 'thank you.' After that experience, he and Penny decided dealing with Bruce was too stressful. He had been spoiled as a child, being the younger of the two boys, and was often allowed to get away with a lot of mischief. When he'd gotten in trouble, he'd never been taught and was never required to take any responsibility for the outcome. Most of the time, his attitude made it difficult to help him, much less feel sorry for him.

That's why it was so hard for Penny to understand – *this time things were different.* This was not only Bruce's reputation on the line - the *family name* was in jeopardy! THIS HAD TO BE FIXED! Blackmail was not acceptable and was not going to happen to the Munroe family - *Not Now - Not Ever! Not as long as he had anything to do with it*!

Bruce's past indulgences, mostly minor infractions, had been relatively easy to conceal. Time after time, Reddick had come to his aid and had been able to keep his bad behavior from public view, more importantly, from the view of the Old Man. Never before had Reddick been so apprehensive or felt such anxiety. The gravity of this new problem, knowing it had the potential to destroy not only his brother, but also the entire family, was almost more than he could bear. He knew the responsibility to resolve this mess fell to him. He needed some advice, thinking he wouldn't be able to resolve this alone.

Reddick's new car had no trouble climbing the steep grade leading to the Club. The members had bought the old house located off Browning Avenue a year or so back. It was remote and perfectly suited their needs as a place for meetings, card games and social events without drawing any unwanted attention. The membership consisted of prominent businessmen, attorneys and a select few elected and appointed public officials. Long ago they recognized the need for a strong, silent leadership in planning the future of the town. They realized the ordinary citizens probably wouldn't understand why this type of leadership was needed, or why these self-appointed leaders would need to meet in secret - behind closed doors. Resolving situations such as this one seemed, in Reddick's mind, to justify both.

The Club members had previously discussed the problems the 'Odd Couple' had been causing in town. Their record shop was the most popular hangout for the local teens, and on weekends Main Street had all but turned into a circus. There was an undercurrent of questionable behavior and rebellion, especially from the older ones. A few ideas as to a solution had been thrown around, but most of the suggestions were considered too drastic and had been dismissed without serious discussion. It continued to be a complicated matter, and the members hadn't been in any hurry to give it much thought or attention until it became absolutely necessary. That all might change with this early morning meeting.

Reddick pulled into the drive and saw that the Chief of Police and one of his attorney friends had already arrived. The Judge and another of the club members were following and pulled in behind him. To his knowledge, a meeting had never been called at this hour and he knew his friends were going to be a little more than anxious to learn about his emergency. They'd hardly cleared the door before a flurry of questions was shot at him. He tried to pacify the group until he could at least get the coffee started.

Once the pot was perking and the gentlemen had seated themselves around the small table, Reddick began to explain the purpose of his early morning call.

He repeated to the group much of the information that Bruce had relayed to him during their pre-dawn discussion. Reddick explained that Bruce's trouble had started a year or so back when he was invited to a party. He'd only been with the family practice a few years and had us believing he was on the straight and narrow since his return from college. Bruce told me the party was wild... booze, drugs and free-for-all sex. He got so wrapped up in the erotic experience, he hadn't thought about who was pay-ing for the booze and drugs. It hadn't even dawned on him the guest list was made up mostly of teenagers and young adults from the wealthiest and most prominent families in the county. At the time, and being under the influence, he hadn't acknowledged to himself any real danger, even though there were several underage teenagers there who were 'putting-out' for the alcohol and drugs.

The situation quickly started to spin out of control. The combination of all the contraband and uninhibited sex made it difficult for anyone to imagine there was anything more sinister going on... only a few of the guests knew or even suspected the entire affair was be-ing photographed. Though some of the partygoers were there only to make for a convincing evening, the parties would prove to be very expensive for a few of the more prominent guests.

Reddick slowly continued, "Yesterday afternoon, an ordinary, legal sized envelope was delivered by express mail to the firm. The envelope was addressed to Bruce Munroe, Attorney at Law, and on the front was stamped **Personal and Confidential**. Bruce told me that when he opened the envelope, a dozen glossy prints fell out. When he realized what he was looking at, he immediately closed his office door and called to the secretary to cancel his remaining appointments for the day. He took the prints, a bottle of bourbon from his desk and walked out the back door. In the wee hours of the morning, he turned up on my doorstep."

The weight of the silence around the table was almost unbearable. Each of the men knew the time had come to take action, but they were no more ready now than they'd been when they first heard that the faggots were corrupting the local teenagers. It was amazing to this group that the townspeople had seemed to *accept* the weird lifestyle of these two, and had exhibited no repulsion to it whatsoever. This was not the direction these professionals wanted *their* town to follow.

Finally, breaking the long silence, the Chief of Police spoke up, "Was there a letter or any demand with the pictures?"

The question seemed to rouse Reddick out of his own deep thoughts about a possible solution. "Only a note to the effect the pictures and negatives *should* be worth a lot of money to the *right* person. It didn't state how much money or even who to pay. Bruce said he was positive where the pictures were taken, but he couldn't be so sure about who could have sent them. He seemed to think Stevens was too much of a gentleman to do something like this, but he wouldn't put it past Gillespie."

The Chief, being a chain smoker, lit up yet another cigarette. "It would be hard to say that a crime's been committed since there's no *real* demand for money. Even if we knew for sure who the sender was, maybe he just wanted your brother to have a little souvenir... maybe a memento for old times' sake. The worst-case scenario is it could be just the beginning... it could get very embarrassing and very ugly. Maybe we should take care of it before it snowballs into more than we can handle," he continued, as the smoke created a bluish gray haze over the table.

Reddick noticed that the other members had been more reserved than usual the entire morning.... even Bo was quiet. A month or so ago, he would have jumped right onboard with anything that could have been done about these queers. He was more than ready to do something then. However, at the time, he didn't indicate that it was personal and certainly didn't give any details. Maybe Bo *had* been implicated but was too embarrassed to admit to anything, especially to us. Besides, at that time, the collective thought of the group was "we weren't directly affected and didn't want to get involved until we were."

After the blunt and rather coldly professional remark by the Chief, Reddick was suddenly having second thoughts about airing this dirty laundry before his colleagues. He now felt a tinge of regret that he'd called this meeting at all. "Maybe we should give this matter some thought over the weekend," Reddick said. "We can get back together Monday night and discuss this problem further. By then, hopefully we can come up with some way to fix this once and for all."

Reddick had just thought of a possible solution to his problem, as well as ending the ongoing bad influence on the local kids.

The coffee pot was drained without a lot more discussion of the problem and they shook hands, as they usually did, before filing out the door. Reddick was confident that his friends wouldn't discuss anything they'd been told. There was an honor code of sorts that existed among the members... an unspoken bond of trust and respect. Some of these men were, like him, second generation, but the Chief of Police and the Judge were there in the beginning when Reddick's father started the Beacon Club. Still, he was a little embarrassed he'd called the meeting. During the discussion, he got a sense from some of the members that they would prefer to distance themselves from this entire matter. Had he been thinking clearly, the possibility of an easy solution would have occurred to him before now. He hoped that when he next saw his friends, the problem would be behind them.

****

Reddick arrived at his office a little earlier than usual... after all, his day had begun hours ago. As their secretary had yet to arrive, he made a beeline for his file cabinets. Earlier at the Club, he had remembered a client who he'd represented a few years back. Unfortunately, the guy was as 'guilty as hell,' but due to the combination of excellent representation and a brilliant plea bargain, he was sentenced to only a few years at the State prison. If this case had gone south, he could have been a permanent fixture there, and the poor sap knew it. *Reddick actually had a client 'doing time' who was 'grateful' to him for his representation.* He must admit this was a first. Thinking back to that final day of trial, Reddick recalled the last thing his client said to him before they led him away, "Man, you did alright... I owe you. When I get out, if you ever need anything, anything at all, just call. I won't be hard to find."

After a few minutes of searching, he put his fingers on the file. As he scanned the sentencing page, his eyes fell on the projected release date. According to this, he should be out, Reddick thought. After a call to a friend who had access to the actual prison records, his former client's release was quickly confirmed. In addition, Reddick was able to obtain addresses and contact phone numbers that had been provided to his parole officer. It took only a few calls to schedule a meeting.

Within thirty minutes their secretary had arrived and cheerfully brought in the morning newspaper and a cup of coffee. Today, even the Tribune couldn't hold a candle to what was going on in his personal life. He'd barely finished the front page when the secretary returned with the schedule. Reddick had been so consumed with his personal dilemma that he'd given little thought to what might be required of him today. When he glanced down at the list, he swallowed hard and only shook his head.

"You might have time for lunch if you carry a peanut butter sandwich in your pocket," she said almost in a giggle, trying to make light of the morning. She knew something was bothering Reddick, but said nothing. Not being the kind to pry, she knew she'd find out in time.

****

In addition to the usual tasks of returning client calls and drafting assorted legal documents, Reddick had several unexpected motions to be dictated and filed with the Clerk's Office. As is generally the case with legal matters such as these, time was of the essence. Usually, his work was only time consuming and required some concentration, but today, the tasks seemed to be a lot more difficult. Reddick was so intent on resolving his own problems, harnessing his attention to focus on someone else's was a bit more difficult.

He generally enjoyed his line of work, since it allowed him certain indulgences and a privileged lifestyle. However, today the unexpected workload and added time constraints had reduced the enjoyment to a simple motivation to survive. As the hours seemed to drag on, he was getting even more anxious about what he had yet to do. He had gotten his second wind about the time he picked up his briefcase and headed out the back door toward the parking lot. It was finally time to get on to the more important business of the day.

****

Normally, the mountain climate was very mild. Unfortunately, this July hadn't been that normal and the heat seemed reluctant to give way to the usual cool evening breezes. A rain shower seemed to be the only hope for relief.

The combination of a sleepless night and a day full of deadlines should have taken its toll, but Reddick only felt an unrelenting anxiety as he thought about the events of the past twenty-four hours and the task that lay before him.

The drive to Ashton was uneventful, aside from the purpose. Reddick was relatively familiar with the downtown area, especially around the Federal Courthouse... he'd been there often and could navigate through the streets pretty well. Though only a few blocks away from the Courthouse, the address he'd been given seemed to be in a different world. With only minor difficulty he located the street, and knew the number he was looking for couldn't be too much further. He easily spotted the building, but after looking around at the neighborhood, he was reluctant, but pulled his new car up to a front parking space anyway. He got out and turned to carefully close and lock the driver's door. He glanced around again, and then turned his attention back to admire the shiny finish on his new Mercedes coupe. Confident that he wouldn't be recognized, he went inside and asked the desk clerk for the room number for Frederick Johnson, his old client.

Freddie answered the door after only one knock... he had expected Reddick to be there much earlier. Worried since the morning phone call, he couldn't figure why Mr. Munroe would be looking for him. He remembered what he'd said to his attorney in the courtroom on that last day of court, and under his breath, he was hoping he wouldn't live to regret the offer of help he'd made. He had just finished his time at the State prison and had no intention of ever going back. Freddie reached out and firmly shook Reddick's hand, immediately patting him on the back as though he was glad to see him. He then introduced him to the unsavory character who was there with him in the room.

"What's this all about, you needin' to talk to me so urgent and all?" Freddie asked.

Reddick's reply was almost mechanical, "Let's go get something to eat and I'll tell you all about it."

****

Driving home, Reddick felt as though a weight had been lifted from his shoulders. Just as he was mentally congratulating himself, an unexpected chill passed over him. What kind of miracle would he have to perform to keep his father from ever finding out about this mess? Everyone knew who was still in charge... just like *"The Godfather"* he still ruled this family with an iron fist! The Old Man would permanently disown Bruce for getting himself into such a disgraceful predicament... putting the family name at risk like this would not be acceptable. The Munroe name was well respected, and had been since the very founding of the town. Knowing his father as he did, Reddick would somehow manage to get at least part of the blame for not keeping a closer watch on his kid brother.

After the sudden flash of anxiety had subsided, Reddick tried to console himself with thoughts of resolution. Besides, Freddie talked as if taking care of this little matter would be no problem. Reddick remembered telling him that a *good scare* would be sufficient to dissuade any further action from these two "pansies." With any luck at all, they would close up shop and leave town altogether.

Freddie promised that he'd do just as Reddick had requested, and do it soon. "Just a good scare, no real violence." Reddick was confident that the two 'C-notes' he'd pressed into Freddie's hand were enough incentive to do just as he was instructed ... no more... no less.

Reddick finally felt as though he could breathe a little easier. He was certainly ready for a good night's sleep... maybe even 'till noon tomorrow, since it was Saturday.

The Affair ....

Mike cut his lights as he inconspicuously rolled to a stop on the side street a half block from her house. After looking around at the vacant street, he felt that he hadn't set off any alarms or raised any suspicions. Though they had been meeting secretly like this for a month or so, he continued to be a little nervous. Carefully planning his travel time so as to be only a few minutes early, his heart had already begun to pound with anticipation. He combed through his hair again as he anxiously watched his rearview mirror. Having to wait only a couple of minutes, he saw Beckey walking slowly around the corner toward his car. With the streetlight at her back, he easily recognized her shapely silhouette.

Though she was more than a few years younger than he, the physical attraction was immediate and definitely mutual. Mike remembered falling for her the first time he looked into her eyes; he was completely infatuated, stumbling all over himself... which certainly was not characteristic for him.

She appeared to be much older and certainly more mature than her actual years. They had the "age-differ-ence" discussion shortly after they began dating, and the only ones who seemed to be having a problem with it were her parents. Mike Franks was well aware that they not only disapproved of him because they considered him too old for her, but also because he had been married and re-cently divorced. He realized that he had begun this new relationship with two strikes against him, at least as far as her parents were concerned.

As Beckey opened the car door and gracefully slid onto the seat beside him, he noticed that something in her manner was just not the same.

"Hey Baby, have any trouble getting out?" he asked as he reached for her.

She made no reply, but seemed to relax completely when he pulled her close to him. He felt her damp tears against his face as he gently kissed her – again and again. He continued to hold her closely, feeling every breath and every heartbeat. The smell of her... her hair was com-pletely intoxicating to him. He had never before experi-enced the feeling that he could not get close enough... he had never felt this way about anyone before.

"What is it, Baby? What's wrong with my Angel?" he softly crooned.

Mike assumed that she had been quarrelling with her parents. She had told him a couple months back, that they had strictly forbidden her to see him again – there had been several heated arguments. This was the reason for the clandestine rendezvous; she was not supposed to see him, much less be with him.

Beckey's father was extremely successful. He had started working in the men's clothing industry at an early age, and after years of hard work, saving and making a name for himself; he now owned a chain of prestigious Men's Shops in the Southeast. Mike knew all about the rags-to-riches story, because in addition to being Beckey's father, he was also his employer. He knew that proving himself to Mr. Jordan was not going to be easy, but he felt in time, his honest and sincere intentions toward his daughter, Miss Rebecca Jordan would become evident and he would win her father over.

An unexpected squeal of tires and a flash of car lights startled them, interrupting their embrace. They quickly sat up and assumed the posture of driver and passenger. After the vehicle passed, Mike started the engine and slowly moved away from the curb and headed for a more private location. He, being the smooth operator that he had always been, knew them all.

Mike drove several blocks before they were out of the up-scale neighborhood of Towne Forest. He continued his drive across town and onto a back street he knew to be safe and usually deserted. He smiled to himself as he thought about the last time he and Beckey were here. Flushing with anticipation, he remembered the incredible passion they had shared.

He pulled the car to the curb and once more turned off the headlights. The car windows were down, so Mike felt confident that he would be alerted if anyone happened down their way. There were a few streetlights, so they were not parked completely in the dark.

He turned to Beckey and again they fell together in a passionate embrace. After a few minutes, Beckey slowly pulled back a bit. "What are we going to do, Mike? We just can't go on like this forever, meeting in secret and lying to my parents. I know they suspect something is going on, and this is getting more difficult every day. You know how I feel, I *do* love you," she softly said.

"It's gonna' be alright, Baby," he softly whispered in her ear. "In time they'll understand, they'll see how serious we are about each other. Baby, you know how I feel... they'll just have to accept that we're going to be together, and it doesn't really matter what they think! In time..."

Beckey moved closer to Mike. He had already partially unbuttoned her blouse and the lace on her camisole was exposed.

"Baby, we don't have the luxury of time," she softly whispered to him with her lips on his cheekbone.

It took a few seconds for the reality of what she had said to sink in. Mike pulled his face up from her long, lovely neck and his hands from her well-tanned torso. He sat upright and looked at her seriously and expectantly.

As the tears streamed down her beautiful face, she whispered, "I'm going to have your baby." She waited for his reply. Her eyes did not miss a single twitch or muscle movement.

Mike was dumbfounded. He knew that he couldn't mess up now! It would be a major mistake to screw up what he had so carefully planned for so very long. He faked the biggest smile of his life as he pulled her to him and held her. "I'm the happiest man alive," he softly said with his face buried in her long, blonde hair.

They softly made love, though it was clear that their relationship was now on a new level. Mike tried as best he could to appear as though he was delighted with the news... but the drive back to her parents' neighborhood was awkwardly quiet. He tried hard to act as normally as he possibly could, but the shock of this news had only added to the flood of emotions that were now tumbling around in his head.

He pulled the car over to the curb less than a block down the street from her house. He had thoughtfully planned this so that he could watch her until she was safely inside.

"I love you," he whispered as he pulled her closer to him. "Don't worry... it'll all work out, I promise. I'll take care of it, Baby. Don't worry your pretty little head for a minute, we'll figure it out... I promise," he continued as he gently kissed her.

"When will I see you?" she softly asked.

"Soon...very soon," he whispered. "I have some business to take care of tomorrow, but I'll call you on Monday and we'll set a time."

"Mike," she started as she drew back a bit, "the folks are at me to decide where I'm going to school... they want a decision."

"Do you have to decide this right now?" he hesitantly asked.

"I don't know how long I can put them off - they want me to register next week."

"Where do you want to go to school, Baby?"

" I don't know if I *can* go to school, Mike. Remember - I'm pregnant," she hesitated. "Even if I could, I wouldn't want to go to Chapel Hill or Durham... I just couldn't stand to be that far away from you," she answered tearfully. "Oh, we have so much to talk about and decide... I do love you," she whispered as she snuggled her face into the side of his neck.

"Don't worry, Baby. I'll be back day after tomorrow and we'll talk about everything, I promise," he whispered as he gently caressed her. Turning her face to him, he could see the reflection of the streetlight in her eyes. He passionately kissed her, a long and sensuous kiss that seemed to envelop the soul.

She got out of the car and Mike watched every step that she took until she got to the front door. She paused and looked back for a moment, then slowly turned, went inside and closed the massive door.

Mike started the engine and slowly drove past the house before turning on the headlights. The drive home wasn't nearly long enough for Mike to absorb everything that had happened to him today.

****

Mike had laid across the bed and stared at the ceiling for hours trying to figure how to best resolve his current assortment of problems. He gave the most recent news of the evening little thought since he considered it to be more good news than bad. It was just a hell-of-a-lot sooner than he had planned. His main objective was to be the manager, and someday possibly the owner of the clothing business where he worked. His affection for Beckey, and hers for him, could possibly provide a serious shortcut toward a prominent position in her father's business... simply by becoming a member of her wealthy family.

The problem that was of most concern now involved the blackmail pictures that had been delivered to him earlier that morning. His old friend Vince had probably found out about his relationship with Beckey and was having one of his "fits."

Mike sat up in bed staring into the darkness. He had done so many things in his life that he now regretted. Simply moving to another city had taken care of most of the problems, but not all of them. The parties, drugs and binge drinking had most certainly stopped when he moved to Charlottesville. He smiled to himself when he thought about all the attention he used to get back home and his reputation as the "town stud." Those days were gone forever. He had been trying in earnest to turn over a new leaf. The one thing that he had not been able to shake was his relationship with Vince Stevens – his current and most serious problem.

He thought back to his senior year in school when Vince approached him in the record store. He knew who he was, but being a kid at the time, he had no idea what he was getting into. All he knew back then was if he played along with Vince, he would have access to all the parties, drugs, booze and sex he could handle. What kid stuck in a one-horse town could turn down an offer like that?

He laid back across the bed and sweet thoughts of Beckey flooded his mind. He would deal with the problem of Vince tomorrow.

****

Mike had arrived from Charlottesville on the 3:10 p.m. flight. Since he did not have to collect any luggage, he by-passed that section of the terminal and proceeded directly to the car rental counter. Within thirty minutes he had secured a car and was on his way to meet with his friends.

Twenty minutes later, he was back in the familiar neigh-borhood where his buddy Hank lived. As he made the turn off State Street, he noticed the street before him seemed eerily quiet for a Sunday afternoon. Normally, there would be so many kids playing ball or riding bikes you couldn't stir 'em with a stick; today, however, it seemed deserted. Mike knew it was too hot outside, even for the kids.

He pulled in the drive and parked behind Hank's '57 Chevy, and noticed that Robbie had already gotten there because his blue Pontiac, the *Blue Goose*, was parked un-der a tree at the back of the house. As he turned off the engine, both Hank and Robbie came ambling out the back door. They had been expecting Mike and greeted him with a cold beer. The trio stood outside only a few minutes en-gaging in small talk, before moving back into the kitchen closer to the window fan.

After they each pulled up a chair around the table, Hank turned around and pulled three more beers out of the refrigerator. They popped the caps in unison as Mike began to fill them in on yesterday's events. Hank and Rob-bie didn't appear to be too surprised. After all, they knew him well... they had been his friends since grade school. They knew about all the crap he had done, matter of fact, they had been involved in most of it! They also knew the situation with Vince, and the fact that he refused to let Mike end their relationship... he simply refused to let it go.

Mike knew he could count on his buddies to help him resolve this problem with Vince, as they had never made a secret of their dislike for him. They understood that since Mike could not take a chance on Beckey or her father finding out about this... or anything else about his past for that matter, they had to find a solution to this problem today.

As they started to discuss all the aspects of the pending situation, Hank spoke up. "Suppose you were to just pay Vince the money you owe him, would that get him off your back?"

Robbie quickly jumped into the conversation. "It isn't the money Vince wants. When he paid for those surgeries for Mike, you know he didn't expect to get that money back."

Mike agreed. It was evident that just paying Vince the money he owed him – even if he had it – wouldn't resolve the problem. Vince wanted more than the money... *Vince wanted him*. The thought of his past sickened him. This old man had a lover, but he just could not accept the fact that Mike was no longer interested in him... he had gotten on with his life.

Mike had been told that Vince had started to drink heavily and had constantly blamed everyone around for his humiliation and pain; he was way past rationalization or negotiation. That was the reason he had chosen this particular time to send the explicit pictures. This was his threat! Vince knew that these photographs would not be well received by Mike's fiancée, much less her parents.

With little more discussion, they agreed the only solution, at least as they saw it, would be to get the photos - **all the photos**, hopefully without any confrontation.
Then maybe this showdown would end. They just had to
come up with a plan of exactly how to go about it - *short
of having to kill someone.*

Hank grabbed three more beers 'for-the-road' as they
headed out the back door toward Mike's car.

****

Mike backed out of Hank's drive onto a side street. After a couple of turns he proceeded on State Street, then
turned toward town. Since they felt it unlikely that this
car would be recognized in town, Mike's friends felt in
control, cocky and were ready to follow through on any
course of action that might be required - whatever it may
be. Frankly, Mike's two cronies never imagined getting
into any real trouble... they generally considered out-
landish activities, but talk was usually as far as it had ever
gone. As they approached a busy intersection, both Hank
and Robbie ducked and turned away so that some guys
they knew wouldn't see them.

Mike turned left and continued north on Main. He
slowed considerably when he approached the record shop
owned by Vince and Clarence. Just as Mike had feared,
Clarence's car was parked out front. He usually left it
there when he and Vince were together. Maybe they

would be lucky enough for Clarence to actually be at the shop. Mike had no desire to confront Clarence... he vehemently disliked this "Voodoo Princess" and knew well that the feeling was mutual. What he needed was to find Vince alone so that he could talk some sense into him.

After another turn or two, they found themselves approaching the Stevens' house. Mike slowed the car to get a better view as they rounded the corner. He immediately noted that the blue sedan belonging to Vince's dad was not in the drive.

The next thing that came into view could prove to be an amazing opportunity.

Just how lucky could they get?

The Betrayal ....

The anger in his booming voice was totally consuming. The impression he made with his index finger pressing firmly on Peter's nose left no doubt that he meant business. Angelo did not intend to waste any more time on this loser. He made that evident with his tone. The beads of perspiration rolling across the protruding blood vessels on his temples painted a horrible picture in Peter's mind.

"So the Hillbilly queers owe you money, huh?" Angelo shouted. "Well, I guess you need to take a little trip to visit your faggot friends and get it. I'm going to send Leo here with you, just to make sure you come back. You get that money and be back here Monday – or Leo will be bringing you back in a bag!"

With that, Angelo stormed out the kitchen door, almost tearing the screen off its hinges.

Tears and perspiration rolled down Peter's face, bringing back a flush of the color that had drained when Angelo and his friend Leo first burst into his house. He laid over the table and cradled his head in his hands. His heart was pounding so hard he thought that his head would explode. He thought his body had gone numb, but now he could feel his pulse in the bottoms of his feet. He had never in his life been so terrified. After a few silent minutes he was able to regain his composure enough to breathe again.

The look on Leo's face revealed the shock of witnessing a side of his boss that he had never before seen. Leo had worked for Angelo for some time now, but had never seen him explode like this.

When Leo arranged the loan for Peter a couple months ago, he thought he was doing Peter a favor. Just a short-term loan... the interest was high, but when you can't get immediate money you have to expect that.   When Peter got the loan, he had been confident that he was going to be receiving a sizable sum that had been owed to him for a long time; Gillespie would be sending his mortgage money any day. His friend, Vince Stevens, had promised him faithfully he would see to it.

Peter thought Vince to be his lifelong friend. As children, they were neighbors and Peter idolized him. Even though Vince was older - the same age as Peter's sister, he always craved his attention. He was jealous of his sister's friendship with Vince and didn't understand why he wanted to hang around with her. Vince had taught him so much about being grown up, with real grown up feelings. Peter assumed he and Vince had a special bond, a secret physical bond. He had never gotten over the strong feelings he had for Vince. Those memories flooded back into his mind, not as often as they used to, but they were every bit as powerful.

That bond and friendship may have to take a back seat to what now has to be done. Angelo made it very clear that he wanted his money or else. It wasn't hard to imagine what the "or else" meant.

Leo and Peter were the most unlikely of friends. Leo had come into Peter's office complaining of severe back pain. It seemed that the problem was a dislocated disc, caused from lifting heavy boxes. Leo explained that when large shipments came into the packinghouse, he had to help unload the trucks. This was not his regular job... he was a *collection agent* for his boss, Angelo Bevonnie. He explained how Angelo had been willing to give him a chance to prove his ability when he got out of prison this last time. Jobs were hard to come by, especially if you've been in the joint.

Since Leo happened to be Peter's last patient the day of that first appointment, they began talking. Leo was very rough around the edges. He had experienced some bad breaks in his life and had been in and out of prison first for one thing and then another. Though he was very large and muscular, he didn't seem to be such a bad guy, if you didn't feel threatened or intimidated by his size or his vast array of tattoos... Peter certainly would not intentionally anger him. He wasn't the smartest guy in the world, but he had been trained to follow directions perfectly. Peter came to realize the only thing that he and Leo had in common was they both had served in the Navy.

With a simple adjustment, Leo was already in less pain and began to walk a little straighter. After having a couple more alignments over the next few days, Leo was as good as new. He thought that Peter was magic. He knew nothing about fixing the skeletal system; he only knew what it took to break one... and over the years he had broken his share.

About the time Leo came into his life, Peter had become desperate to get out of the serious financial situation he had slowly slipped into. A few years back he had brought his ailing father up from Carolina so that he could care for him. It was a good idea at the time, but gradually the cost of his support and medications had become enormous. In addition, Peter's wife had become discontented with the situation and decided she needed money to go back to school. These factors, added to the continuing slump his business had suffered, had put Peter in a terrible financial bind. He would have barely been able to make the ends meet even *if* he had been receiving the rent money from his father's house.

In the back of his mind, Peter thought it might prove useful to have an acquaintance that appeared to be of the criminal persuasion, in case he had to go to Carolina to collect his money from Gillespie personally. Of course, Peter only toyed with that idea. As meek and mild natured as he was, he never really would have had the guts to actually do it himself. After he had a few drinks and got to thinking about the situation, getting angry, cursing and threatening was all he was ever likely to do.

****

Leo and Peter had been driving for what seemed to be an eternity, but in actuality it had only been a few hours. The conversation thus far had centered on the fact that Angelo had to be paid *and*, according to Peter's calculations, Gillespie owed him several thousand dollars. They had stopped once for coffee at a roadside dive, but it had been cooked so long they were not able to drink it. Peter asked Leo to stop at the next wide place in the road to try to find a coke.

Just ahead there appeared to be a small store and filling station. Leo whipped in and topped off the tank while Peter went inside. He was glad to get out of the car, stretch his legs and go to the restroom. Just getting a breath of fresh air was a big relief after so many miles cooped up in that smog. Peter did not smoke but Leo certainly made up the difference. The choking smoke layered itself inside the car like a poison. He could smell the smoke on his clothing well after getting out and going inside the filling station. As he passed the cooler on the way to the register to pay for the gas, he removed two large cokes. Anything cold would help to fight the heat.

He had to put some serious thought into exactly what he was going to do when they got to Carolina. He had blown Leo a lot of hot air about how all this money had been taken from him, and in reality it had. But the situation was not quite the way he had painted it to Leo. He could never hurt Vince, nor could Peter ever think he had anything to do with this. It was all Gillespie! He was the one taking the rent and not paying the mortgage with the money. He was the one lying to Vince, telling him that he had been taking care of it. He really did not want anyone to get hurt... except maybe Gillespie.

After they had stretched their legs and Peter gave Leo his coke, they returned to the car. Much to Peter's relief, it had aired out a little. At least the haze had dissipated so as to provide visibility through the front windshield.

They pulled back onto Highway 27. Leo started to question Peter about what they might expect when they got to Carolina. He wanted details, as he was already trying to figure out what must be done and the easiest way to do it. Peter felt he didn't have much time to figure out how to get this money and get back home without anyone getting hurt, especially Vince.

Even though Leo and Peter had been friends for several months now, it was very clear that Leo's allegiance was to his employer. Make no mistake: Peter knew that Leo would not be his ally against Angelo. If they failed, Leo would, no doubt, do as he had been instructed. It was clear that Leo admired Angelo, but more importantly, he also feared him. Angelo had made it clear that Leo was going along to assist, or even do the dirty work for Peter. Anything less than a successful completion of this assignment would subject Leo to suffer the same fate that Angelo had threatened for Peter.

****

The hours and the miles seemed to have little affect on Peter. His mind was in overdrive. The anxiety and fear had almost made him tireless. He had been racking his brain trying to come up with a plan of action. He knew that if he could come up with something, Leo would follow his lead and hopefully no one would get hurt. The biggest problem he could see was a matter of practicality. They would be getting into town in the wee hours of Sunday morning. Peter knew the chances of Gillespie having thousands of dollars just lying around on a Sunday were not very good. And just as important, what were the chances that he could even get it? Gillespie certainly was not expecting this visit and had no idea that Peter would be knocking on his door, much less with such an intimidating companion.

The thoughts of his desperate situation convinced him he really should not care where or how Gillespie got the money, **just as long as he did**. After all, this whole matter was Clarence Gillespie's fault. But in reality, he had rationalized why he *should* care that Gillespie comes up with the money. If he doesn't, someone might wind up dead. Peter could not stand the thought of Vince getting hurt, but he most feared the consequences that he himself might have to face on Monday when he was to meet with Angelo.

The pair had been driving under the cover of darkness for quite a few hours. They had talked about every subject imaginable, but a plan had yet to materialize. Peter was getting more anxious now, as they were within an hour of their destination.

"I think the most sensible thing to do would be to get a place to stay for tonight," Peter finally announced to Leo. "In the morning we can find Gillespie and even Vince, if we need to. I think we would have a better chance of finding them tomorrow," he continued.

Leo was a little hesitant to agree with Peter's plan. He just wanted to whack this Gillespie character, get the money and head back to Indiana. The sooner he could smooth things over with Angelo, the better. This whole affair, together with the possibility that maybe Angelo was mad at him for this, was making him very nervous.

The situation put Leo at a disadvantage. He was in a strange place and had no clue where to find these people, so he had no choice but to agree to Peter's plan to rest a few hours and get a fresh start in the morning.

There weren't many places you could check in at any hour without making a prior reservation. However, the last couple of years, when coming to Carolina, Peter had stayed at Pervis Cottages on the south end of town. Since his house had been rented, his options as far as a place to stay had been limited. Besides, this place was a little more flexible than most. It was the kind of place that asked no questions if you paid cash. They didn't even require guests to sign a register – this would work out perfectly for Peter and Leo.

Highway 25 between Ashton and Peter's hometown was completely deserted at this hour of the morning. They drove straight through town and only slowed in the curve just before the cottages on the left. As Leo turned into the drive, Peter said, "It would be better for you to go in and get the room. I've been here before and it would be best if no one recognized me." Leo agreed. No one would know him since he had never been in this hick town before.

Though Peter had been entertaining various thoughts about what needed to be done, he had not worked out a plan of exactly how to proceed. One thing he had decided though, was that he needed to be invisible. If bad turned to worse, he did not need to be seen in town this particular weekend.

Leo came back to the car with a key and cabin number. He slowly drove past the Office and backed the car up next to the cabin. He figured that no one knew his car but didn't want to advertise his Indiana plates. The two gathered what little luggage they had brought and went inside the tiny structure. There were two half beds, a table with a couple of chairs, a TV and a humming window fan. They were in agreement that they were most impressed with the fan. Almost in unison, they each threw their bag in a chair and flopped across a bed.

Soon, Leo was fast asleep and snoring in time with the strains of the noisy fan. Peter only laid there staring into the darkness. He could never remember the mountains having weather like this... *everything* was different. His whole life had gone to hell in a hand basket and he felt he could do little about it! In just a few hours, he knew he was going to have to pull a rabbit out of a hat or Leo would resolve this issue for him. What a terrifying thought!

Peter let Leo sleep as long as possible. The sun was up and so were the temperature and the unbearable humidity. He had heard people stirring outside the cabin next door when he got up to go to the bathroom. The loud squeak of the closing door must have aroused Leo from his slumber and back into consciousness. When Peter came out of the bathroom, Leo was digging through his bag looking for a clean shirt and his toothbrush.

"Do you want the shower first?" Leo asked as he looked up at Peter.

"No, you go ahead, I'll make us a cup of coffee," Peter replied. While the coffee was brewing, Peter was thinking about the ominous day that lay before them.

After an hour of multiple cups of coffee and a refresh-ing shower, the two were back in the car. They had decid-ed not to check out of the cabin just yet. After they took care of this pending matter, they might want to shower and catch a few more hours of sleep before beginning the long trip back.

They slowly made their way down the drive past the Office. The last thing they needed was to attract any at-tention. Peter directed Leo's turns after they reached the end of the drive. He knew that there would be less chance of him being seen if they took the side roads to Gillespie's house. Hopefully, they would have to go no further.

There were few cars on the road. Peter figured that it was partly due to it being Sunday, but mostly due to the heat. As Leo rounded the curves at the Country Club, he asked Peter where they were headed and exactly what his plan was.

" We're not far from Gillespie's house," Peter stated. "With any luck, we may have a good chance of catching him there. Sunday afternoons, he's normally either at home, at the shop, or with Vince."

One turn off Fifth Avenue and they were almost in Gillespie's front yard. Leo slowed to give Peter a chance to get a good look at the place. As luck would have it, they were the only ones on the street... not a car to be seen at the house, or any sign of life, for that matter.

Peter told Leo to circle the block. They turned left when they came back out on Fifth Avenue and traveled only a dozen blocks to Main Street. At the intersection, Peter glanced across the street and to his right. There, in front of the record shop, sat Gillespie's car. Leo crossed the intersection and slowly turned into the alley behind the storefronts.

"Stop here," Peter directed. " If he's here, he'll be at the back of the shop. I'll go look for inside lights and try to get him to come to the door."

Peter was not out of Leo's sight for a moment.

"There's no one here," Peter shrugged as he returned to the car.

"Are you sure?" Leo asked.

"Lights would be on in the back. You can see all the way to the front of the store... there's no one here," he mumbled as he got in and closed the car door.

"What now?" Leo asked expectantly.

The next place on the list was the last place in the world that Peter wanted to take Leo.

"At the end of the alley, turn left," Peter said, as he felt his heart sinking.

He gave turn-by-turn directions to Leo to get to Maple Street where Vince lived with his father. He then asked him to drive past Vince's house, explaining that by doing so they could see if anyone was there.   Depending on what or whom they found, they would be better able to know what to do.

Leo did just as Peter instructed. When they got to the bend in the street, he slowed. Peter knew that Vince's father drove a dark blue Ford sedan. Peter was somewhat relieved when he saw it wasn't there... the only vehicle in the drive belonged to Vince. A cold chill ran down Peter's back.

"Go around the block. We can hide the car behind my house, and walk through the back yard."

Leo again did as he was instructed. He slowly pulled his car into the drive and around to the back of Peter's house. They got out and quietly let themselves in a back window. The house was completely devoid of anything except trash. Peter had noticed the foreclosure notice tacked to the front door when they first passed by.

"What a mess," Peter said. "This was a nice house when my family lived here. My Mother would turn over in her grave if she could see it now."

Seeing the disappointment and sorrow in Peter's face, Leo spoke up, "Yeah, this is nasty. Someone should have at least cleaned up all this trash." With that, he walked over and opened the door to the front closet. There, propped in a corner, was a pole with a metal fork on the end. "What's this?" he asked as he tossed it toward Peter.

Peter recognized the frog gig from his distant past... a pleasant memory flashed through his mind. He remembered as a young man, he and his father, along with several other male members from the neighborhood, would go gigging in the spring of each year. Then around Christmas time, the gigging participants and their families would gather to have a bountiful shrimp and frog leg supper. It was an annual community event and an occasion that everyone looked forward to... life was much simpler then.

Leo interrupted Peter's thoughts as he turned to go back to the window where they had entered. Leo climbed through the window and Peter followed him, still clinging to the gig in his left hand. After clearing the window, he realized what he had done and started to lean the gig against the house.

Leo turned to him. "You might want to bring that with you."

Leo could tell by the expression on Peter's face that the reality of the situation had finally struck. The color continued to fade from his face as he watched Leo go to the trunk of the car and pull out a short-barreled gun. He fumbled for extra cartridges, which he stuck in his trouser pockets.

"Let's get this done and head on back," Leo said as he quietly closed the trunk.

Together they started across the back yard toward Vince's house.

Unlikely Association ....

It was already mid-afternoon. The forecast for a possible shower had again not materialized. It seemed that there would be no relief, no end to this heat wave. The high humidity, unusual for this temperate climate, just added to the torture.

Shirley had tried to relax in a chair pulled up in front of the window where she had placed a box fan. She lived on the south side of the apartment building and sometimes she got the benefit of a breeze coming up the valley. There were a few large trees on that side which helped to make the temperature a few degrees cooler. Even a few degrees were a blessing in this sweltering heat.

She must have dozed off. Startled, she thought she heard a faint knock on her door. She froze. She really was not sure that she had heard anything. Quickly she moved from her chair and turned the fan off so that she could hear more clearly. After about ten seconds, she heard the faint knock again, and this time someone called her name.

She took a deep relaxing breath when she recognized the voice as being her neighbor, Mrs. Cole.

"Just a minute," she replied, as she quickly made her way to the bedroom to get her blouse. Since she had not been expecting anyone, she had shed as many layers as she could in an effort to beat the heat.

Before opening the door, Shirley peered through the "peep hole" just to be sure that it was her neighbor. One could never be too careful! Satisfied that Mrs. Cole was alone, Shirley removed the security chain and turned the dead bolt. Upon opening the door, Mrs. Cole just stood there looking apologetic for the interruption. She made no movement to enter. Without hesitation she stated her reason for being there - she had been asked to deliver a message.

Without emotion Mrs. Cole relayed the message. " Mr. Gillespie called. He said it was imperative that he speaks with you as soon as possible. He asked that you call him at Mr. Stevens' house as soon as you can. It was an urgent matter and of the utmost importance."

Having completed her mission, Mrs. Cole turned to go back to her apartment. Almost as an afterthought, she turned to Shirley. "You can use my phone if you like," she said almost begrudgingly.

"Yes, thank you," Shirley replied as her mind was spinning with worry and curiosity. "I'll be right there," she said as she closed the door. She moved to the end of the sofa where her pocketbook sat and reached inside to retrieve her book of numbers. She rarely called Vince's number, and never at his house. What could this possibly be about? Had Clarence and Vince finally had it out over Mike? Had someone gotten hurt? But still, why would he be calling me?

Shirley stepped in front of the mirror. She hurriedly brushed through her hair and straightened her blouse collar while sliding on her shoes. Fumbling with her keys and the book, she was quickly out the door.

A short walk down the hall and Shirley was knocking at Mrs. Cole's door. It was immediately opened and Shirley went inside. She had been there many times before, so silently she just went directly to the phone.

Shirley knew that she would have to be careful of what she said. Even though Mrs. Cole was not in the room, Shirley knew that she was close enough to hear every word of her conversation.

Cradling the telephone receiver between her cheek and shoulder, Shirley quickly flipped the pages in her book to the telephone numbers. There not very many listings on this page. She dialed the number. After only one ring, she immediately recognized Clarence's voice at the other end of the line. He sounded frantic; she knew something was definitely wrong.

Clarence was almost hysterical, but through his excitement, he tried to explain what he wanted. He kept asking Shirley if she understood. He was in too much of a hurry to be concerned with coded conversation. He just wanted to make sure that Shirley had understood the gravity of his dilemma. He indicated to her that he had no idea how serious this situation might become. Shirley had never heard Clarence talk like this and it scared her... she had never heard him sound so fearful.

Shirley promised she would come as soon as she could, bring as much as she had on hand, as well as all she could get on such short notice. She told Clarence she would meet him on the old River Road where they had met for the exchange before. He agreed to the location and ended the call with:

"Just - please - hurry."

She slowly returned the receiver to the cradle and thanked her neighbor for delivering the message and for the use of her phone. She struggled to hide the anxiety she felt after hearing Clarence's desperate plea for help.

She well remembered the last emergency Clarence had created for himself. About six months ago, she was with Vince, Clarence and several of their other friends partying at a club in South Ashton. Clarence had made a deal with a local supplier for some drugs and had tried to leave without settling his account. The dealer was not amused... very coolly he drew back and whacked Clarence across the shin with a ball bat. His leg snapped like a dried twig. The commotion this created in the parking lot immediately attracted a rough looking crowd, so the guys quickly helped

Clarence to the car and got him back across the county line to a hospital closer to home.

Shirley thought Clarence surely would have learned you don't play games with these people. His constant pain and still walking with crutches should be enough reminders.

Shirley slowly and cautiously walked back down the hallway to her apartment, ever mindful of anyone she might meet by chance, or that might be loitering there. When she was safely inside she quickly closed and locked the door.

She had to collect her thoughts. How could she come up with the kind of money and amount of drugs to get Clarence off the hook this time? It was late Sunday afternoon, most of her money was in the bank and she had already delivered a good portion of the Thursday supply. She did have the money from the sales and about a fourth of the supply left. Luckily, she knew someone close by who would have a small amount of cocaine on hand and maybe would trust her for it until her next shipment arrived at 11:00 p.m. that night. She knew she could replace it then.

Shirley quickly packed what she had on hand, together with all the cash she had from the sales in a small black tote. She grabbed her handbag and made sure to place the book back inside. She then closed and locked the apartment door and hurried down the hallway. She raced down the staircase to the back door of the apartment building toward the parking lot.

When she opened the door of her blue Ford Fairlane, the heat from inside felt like she was entering an oven. It was unbearable so she quickly rolled down all the windows to try to cool the car. She started the engine, backed out into Hilliard and was quickly at the intersection of Biltmore Avenue. After traveling several blocks south, Shirley swerved into the parking lot of the Townhouse Bakery to use the pay phone.

She pulled out the small book and flipped to the information on the inside back cover. She put a dime in the pay phone and quickly dialed the number of a small time local dealer. The phone rang twice and a gruff and surly voice quickly answered with a, "Yeah??"

"This is Shirley. I need a score... can we meet?"

" When?" the man asked.

"Now," she answered. "Bring all you have; I'll explain when I see you."

"Be there in 10 minutes," he replied.

Shirley pulled across the street into the A&P parking lot. With the unbearable heat, there wasn't much traffic there late on Sunday afternoon. Everyone was at the local pools and lakes, or at he Recreation Park trying to stay as cool as possible. She didn't have to wait long.

The dealer pulled into the space beside her, headed in the opposite direction, so his door was next to hers. She had done business with this guy many times before, but only on a cash basis and not in the middle of the day. She explained her situation and after careful consideration he agreed to trust her for the drugs. They agreed to meet at this same location at 11:30 p.m. that night for payment. He made it very clear to Shirley that it would be in her best interest not to try anything funny. She assured him that this emergency was a onetime thing and after today, it would be business as usual.

Shirley was first to pull out of the parking lot and headed south on Biltmore. The dealer was right behind her, only he headed north. He traveled a few blocks and then turned around to follow Shirley at a safe distance.

Soon she was out of Ashton and headed to her rendezvous with Clarence. She was so deep in her own thoughts of what she might be getting into; she paid little attention to the traffic behind her.

From Ashton, it was almost a straight shot to the appointed meeting location. The drive was long, but not complicated. This left plenty of time for Shirley to try and imagine just what she would be facing when she got there. Just in case things got out of hand, she took the small book of numbers from her handbag and put it in a small pocket under the driver seat. She had crafted the secret pocket when she had first gotten the car. She figured that it would come in handy one day, and she guessed that this just might be that day. To the right people, it could be a lot more valuable than anything she might be dealing now.

Shirley was congratulating herself on how clever she had always been. So cautious and calculating were her everyday actions no one really knew her or knew what she was all about. No one knew that she led a secret life.

She had met Clarence a few years back in Ashton at a club called Chez Paul. She and Clarence had experimented with a relationship, but it was a short-lived physical attraction that was over almost as soon as it had begun. They both realized that a business partnership stood to be abundantly more fruitful. She knew they could use each other, so consequently they became good friends and business partners instead of lovers. Besides, Clarence already had a lover. He had been passionately in love with and insanely jealous of Vince Stevens for many years. Shirley would never come between Clarence and Vince because he had made their most profitable business venture possible.

It was easy for Vince to get the socially elite to attend his parties. After all, he was well liked and everyone who knew him thought he was a gentleman. He was a little naïve and definitely too trusting, but that was his nature. Clarence and Shirley had not intended to use Vince, but thought what he didn't know wouldn't hurt him.

Shirley had been providing the drugs for the parties for a long time, but by chance, another opportunity to make money had presented itself. It was revealed when Vince found another way to entertain some of his party guests. He took up photography so he could take their pictures during the parties. These select guests knew the pictures were being taken and thought nothing of it, in fact they were amused. These were not the kind of pictures that could be taken to the local drug store or corner photo lab for developing, so when Clarence offered to have a friend develop the explicit pictures, Vince agreed. He was unaware that Shirley was that friend.

Vince had no idea that Shirley and Clarence had been taking advantage of the party atmosphere... they had been exploiting some of the guests behind the scenes. They had seen the opportunity and had put their plan into action a few months earlier. Shirley had already begun to secure her financial future.

As she passed the road leading to the plant where she worked the evening shift, she almost laughed out loud. She thought how perplexed the gate guard appeared every Thursday when she asked him to keep her drugs until she got off at midnight. He was such a fool to think she was such a naive little flower... that she was so afraid someone might take her needlepoint or knitting! He repeatedly would tell her to lock her car and anything she left inside would surely be safe. The idiot never even thought to ask what was in the package, not that she would tell him - the truth anyway. As long as she continued to park in the same spot, under the big light, she felt that if anyone came looking for her supply, the guard would spot them before they could break into her car. How brilliant on her part that the drugs would be with the guard and completely out of danger all the while.

She was confident she had duped everyone. No one had any idea she soon would have as much money as she would ever need. Just a couple more successful years and she could afford to leave these pitifully slow, stupid people. She wanted to go back to Charleston or even Atlanta to live...to be anywhere but this dead hellhole! Working with Clarence had already been more profitable than all the drug deals she had done in the last year and a half. She smiled to herself as she continued on her mission to help her partner.

She slowed as she passed the intersection of Fanning Bridge Road. She quickly scanned the passing vehicles to see if any of her co-workers might be in the area - not that any one she worked with would even know who she was. She kept a very low profile and seriously doubted any of those fools would even recognize her.

Driving on, she was getting further out in the country and nearer her destination. It was surprising how quickly the terrain had turned rural. This area was known to be some of the richest farming soil in the region... it was certainly well fertilized. Today the aroma was simply overwhelming! Shirley hoped that what she smelled was not what she was driving directly into.

As she turned off the main highway onto a side road, she did not even look into her rearview mirror. The memories of her past few years here and the questions of what might happen when she got to the meeting place, had temporarily consumed her. She had given no thought of being followed, so she took no notice of the vehicle that had been well behind her for the last half hour or so.

Shirley took a right turn about 500 yards after leaving the paved road. Though she could be seen from the main road, most of the traffic would not notice anyone there due to the proximity to the bridge. This narrow lane used to be the old road across the river and now was just a dead end... it was used only for farm trucks and tractors. The rich soil on either side had been plowed and planted, though the intense heat of the summer had taken its toll on the crops. Shirley noticed that the blackberries near the edge of the trees were ripe, so she made a mental note to call her friend and set up a time to pick and preserve them.

As she neared the end of the road, she was surprised to see that no one was there. She had expected Clarence to be there before her... he said he would be waiting - she should come as soon as possible. He must have been delayed.

This puzzled Shirley. She pulled her Ford Fairlane down to the end of the road and turned off the engine to wait for him. After a few minutes she got out of the car and walked a few feet to an over-laden berry bush. She had never been able to resist the sweet flavor of the ripened fruit.

She amused herself with the thought that if Clarence didn't show up, at least the entire trip was not a waste.

It turned out Shirley wouldn't have to wait very long.

Black Monday ....

Reddick felt rested after his event-free weekend. After everything that had happened in the wee hours of Friday and the rest of that nightmarish day, this past weekend was a much-needed blessing.

He had talked with Bruce mid-day Saturday and told him the situation was under control. He didn't feel premature in telling him he need not worry and could, in fact, rest easy about the entire affair.

It was exactly this type of morning that made Reddick enjoy his chosen profession. His Monday had been very productive thus far. He had dictated a few letters that were only a few days past due. In addition, he had filed a Custody Complaint and dictated an Answer. All in all, things were going extremely well for a Monday.

As Reddick was walking back into the office from a business lunch with a prospective client, the main line rang at the receptionist's desk. Though he could hear only one side of the conversation, he knew it was someone

important and they needed to talk to him - *immediately.*
He told his secretary, Elsie, he would take the call in his
office. He quickly went in and closed the door. As he sat
down, he hesitated before lifting the receiver. A multi-
tude of possible crises flashed through his mind. What
now? What was going to ruin the makings of a very good
day?

He lifted the receiver, "Reddick Munroe."

"Where are they? What in the hell have you done?"
was the frantic reply at the other end of the line.
*"They've been reported missing. What the <u>hell</u> have
you done?"*

Reddick instantly recognized the voice at the other end
of the line as that of the Chief of Police. His blood ran
cold at the accusation. "Slow down, Chief, and tell me
what you're talking about."

"They both were reported missing this morning.
Neither of them showed up for work. You know that can't
be a coincidence! I can't talk now... I'll call you later."
The line went dead. Someone must have walked into his
office, Reddick thought.

His mind started racing at the horrible possibilities.
Damn... just when I thought things were going to settle
down... oh shit, what the hell has happened? I wonder if
Freddie had anything to do with this? Oh my God, what
if he... No... he couldn't have... He was just going to give
them a good scare... No problem, he said... Just a good
scare... *Oh my God, what has he done?*

Bruce had not shown up at the office that morning and Reddick thought that he might have taken a few days off to recuperate from the trauma of last Friday. He then wondered if his absence had anything to do with the Chief's call.

Reddick called to the front desk to tell his secretary that he had an emergency and would not take any calls.

He picked up the phone and dialed Bruce's home number, but got no answer. Then he called Bruce's in-laws to see if his family might be visiting there... struck out again. Reddick didn't even bother to call Mom and Dad, because he knew that Bruce wouldn't dare risk looking into the face of the Old Man after such a fresh episode. His conscience would give him away in a minute.

He felt an urgency to find Bruce - and then try to find out more about the circumstances surrounding the Chief's call. He grabbed his jacket and was out the back door.

Having been unable to reach Bruce on the phone, Reddick drove by his house only to find no car in the drive and no answer at his door. Not knowing where else to look at this time of day, he drove back to the Courthouse to get the scoop on the missing persons. In this town, news traveled by word of mouth long before it hit the press or the radio. Generally, law enforcement kept the 'legal eagles' at the Courthouse up-to-the-minute on anything that happened.

Much to Reddick's dismay, there was nothing new to report. The two men had been reported missing about mid-morning. They were last seen late Sunday after-noon, at different locations and by different people. An alert had been posted, but a search had not yet been initiated.

Reddick went back to the office and pulled the file on Freddie. He started calling numbers... Freddie couldn't be reached and his contacts hadn't seen or heard from him in a couple of days. He called the hotel where he met Freddie and his slimy companion on Friday, only to discover he had checked out.

Son-of-a-bitch! Reddick buried his head in his hands on top of the desk.

****

Reddick was pacing the floor of his office like an ex-pectant father. Unpleasant pictures were flashing through his mind at lightning speed. He thought he had things under control... what in the hell could have happened to make things go so wrong?

Get a grip, he thought to himself. Maybe this has noth-ing at all to do with Freddie or Bruce. I can imagine these two queers have made a lot of enemies in this town. If they were blackmailing my brother, what would make me think that Bruce would be the only target? I shouldn't jump to conclusions until we get a little more informa-tion. Reddick's mind raced as other possibilities flashed before him. Maybe they had a big party last night and are somewhere hung over. Yeah, they'll turn up later today when they find out everyone is looking for them. It could be that Freddie did talk to them yesterday and scared them so bad they went into hiding for a while. Who knows? The important thing now is to keep calm and not get paranoid.

Just as Reddick was about to dial Bruce's number again, the intercom light flashed. He pressed the button, "Yes?"

"It's the Chief on line one," Elsie announced.

"Thanks," he replied and immediately pushed the button for that line.

"Chief, what the heck's going on?" Reddick asked.

"Reddick, tell me you had nothing to do with their disappearance," the Chief started.

"Chief, I swear, I don't know a thing," Reddick replied.

"When I heard the reports about those two faggots being missing and I remembered the conversation at the Club on Friday, I couldn't help but put two and two together. Maybe I jumped to conclusions too quickly, but you can certainly see why I would."

"I understand completely how you could come to that conclusion, Chief, but that was just talk... I don't know a thing about this."

"Well... we haven't learned much since this morning. I did send a couple of detectives over to the record shop to interview one of the clerks who said he'd seen them late yesterday on Little River Road. He said he saw Stevens' car... he was able to ID Stevens as the driver and Gillespie in the front seat with him, but he didn't seem to know the other two passengers."

"Looks like I'm going to have to stick close by until we find these two, so you need to call the guys and postpone our meeting for tonight."

"Fine... I'll call the guys and give them a heads up," Reddick replied.

"I'll keep you posted with any news," the Chief said.

"I appreciate your call... if there's anything I can do, don't hesitate to let me know," Reddick almost mechanically replied.

As he was hanging up, Reddick immediately pushed a button for another phone line. He tried calling Bruce again. This time he got an answer.

"*Hello,*" Bruce's wife answered.

Reddick detected the strain in her voice. "Sandra, is Bruce at home?"

"You know he isn't, Reddick! He hasn't stopped drinking since I saw those horrible pictures on Saturday. I don't know where he is and furthermore, I don't care!" she retorted. "He had best not come around here anymore. I don't want anything to do with that sick bastard!"

"Sandra, now settle down. You know Bruce can do some stupid stuff when he's drinking. He's just going through a rough patch..."

"A ROUGH PATCH, MY ASS!" Sandra interrupted. "Since when did pictures like **that** constitute a *rough patch*? I'm alone at home, eight months pregnant with his baby, and he's out screwing everything that moves! That's a *rough patch*? Give me a break, Reddick."

"I know, Sandra, I know... he's really screwed up this time. Do you know where I can find him?"

"Hell no! And when you find him, **DON'T BRING HIS SORRY ASS BACK HERE!**" she shouted as she slammed down the receiver.

Oh shit, Reddick thought to himself... this is all I need! All hell breaks loose and Bruce has to be the center of attention - *again*. What in the crap am I going to tell the Old Man this time?

He stood up to put on his jacket and the intercom flashed again. Elsie announced, "Line one is for you."

"Reddick Munroe," he answered.

"Mr. Munroe, this is Jimmy down at the Blackbird. I know you're busy and I hate to bother you, but I didn't know what else to do..."

"What can I do for you, Jimmy?" Reddick asked.

"It's your brother Bruce. He's been here passed out drunk since Saturday. I can't get him to leave and I don't know what to do with him. I tried to sober him up yesterday while I was closed, but he'd have none of that. I know your Dad's sick and doesn't need to be bothered with this, so I decided to call you..."

"You did the right thing, Jimmy. I'll be right down to get him. Can you meet me at the back?"

"I'll have him ready and waiting," Jimmy replied.

"Thanks, Jimmy. I owe you." With that, Reddick replaced the receiver and finished putting on his jacket. He called to Elsie that he was leaving for the day and went out the back door.

Damn! A freaking three-ring-circus, he thought to himself as he walked out to the parking lot. Penny is just going to love this!

He got in the car and headed toward Church Street to pick up Bruce.

The Search.......

    Yesterday had been a living hell for Reddick. It proved to be one nightmare after another. Penny was not happy to have Bruce staying at their house again. He was still drinking and whining about Sandra and the freaking "queers." Sandra wouldn't even consider talking to him and if that weren't enough... if the Old Man were to ever hear about all this mess... well, it's scary as hell to even think about!

    Reddick was almost afraid to get out of bed. He caught himself thinking – how much worse could it get? No, he told himself, don't even go there, this is only Tuesday! He finally rolled out of bed and got ready for work. With all that was going on, he still had to go to the office. He remembered it was only yesterday he was thinking how much he enjoyed what he did for a living.

    Maybe it wasn't the job as much as it was facing this miserable situation! Nonetheless, the bills didn't stop just because his world was going to hell!

****

When he got into the office everything was quiet. It was so eerie... it was scary. He thought, *the calm before the storm!*

Elsie brought in a cup of coffee and the <u>Tribune</u>.

"Have you seen this?" she said as she laid the paper face up on his desk. "They still don't have a clue as to what happened to these two characters. I guess the authorities will naturally suspect foul play." With that, she turned and left Reddick to read the small side article for himself.

After absorbing every tidbit of information, Reddick picked up the phone and dialed the Chief's personal line.

When he answered, Reddick returned his greeting with "Good morning. Is there any good news yet?"

"No, I've been here most of the night and nothing has turned up. I was getting ready to go home for a few hours. I'll call you when I come back into the office this afternoon."

"I would appreciate that, Chief," Reddick replied. They said their goodbyes and hung up.

Reddick knew he would be hearing nothing more for a few hours, so he reached into the backlog basket on his desk. He might as well make good use of the time and get some of this work done. He had a closing next week requiring a title search... that should be time consuming enough!

****

By late afternoon, Reddick had made a large dent in the work he should have done days ago. It was almost 5:30 before the Chief got back to him.

"Well, we thought we had found Stevens' car, but it was only a false alarm. A car that matched the description had been abandoned off highway 191 on old River Road. Strange thing though, it's registered to a woman who is also missing. The report was made by her employer when she didn't show up for work yesterday."

"The car was just left there?" Reddick asked.

"Yeah, the keys were in the ignition, windows rolled down and a purse hanging on the door handle. Pretty strange, don't you think? The person who reported the abandoned car had seen it yesterday. They thought somebody would come back later to get it; they usually do. However, when it wasn't gone by today, they got suspicious and gave Ben over at the Sheriff's Department a call. This is really going to be weird if these two situations turn out to be connected. That car was a dead-ringer for the one Stevens drives."

"Chief, guess these guys are just hung over somewhere from one of their drug parties?" Reddick asked.

"Could be, but the regular party people say they haven't seen 'em. I called a guy I know over at the Ashton Department and he said he would ask around over there.

Maybe he can find someone who knows something. I'll give you a call when he gets back to me."

"Thanks a lot for keeping me posted. I just hope they turn up soon... I know you have better things to do than chase around after a couple of queers."

"I'll call you tomorrow," the Chief broke in.

Before hanging up, the Chief said, "Oh, by the way, Reddick, how's your Dad doing? I haven't heard from him in a while."

"He's still hanging in there. He has his good days and bad... but all in all, I guess he's doing as well as can be expected. Thanks for asking, I'll tell him you said 'Hello.'"

"Yes, do that," the Chief replied. Then he hung up.

Reddick felt he had accomplished enough for one day. After all, he didn't want Elsie to think for a minute he was an over-achiever. She might expect him to do this much work every day and he certainly was having none of that. She was worse than his Mother!

He put on his jacket, turned off the light and was almost to the front door when he remembered the newspaper. Going back into his office to pick up the paper, he glanced over at his briefcase... no; he wasn't going to take it home with him tonight. Truth was, he would have his hands full with Bruce and Penny at each other's throats.

Ahhh, ain't life great, he thought to himself!

****

Wednesday morning was almost a carbon copy of the day before. The only difference was Reddick had gotten a little more rest. Bruce was drying out and Penny was being a little more civil to everyone. Sandra had not given an inch though... she still would not even consider talking to Bruce. He figured she would probably come around after a little more time.

Reddick remembered how Bruce had mentally picked him clean last night. In fact, he vacuumed every bit of information he could on Stevens and Gillespie. He obviously was not convinced his big brother wasn't somehow involved in this, especially after what he was told on Saturday. That was just before Sandra ran across the pictures in the briefcase.

Reddick had been entertaining the same thoughts about Bruce. He knew he had sufficient motive to do something, but he was just not so sure about the means.

When the paper and the coffee were brought in today, there was a little more to read. The headline in the Tribune stated that Stevens and Gillespie had been officially reported missing. It described the searches and the various interviews with friends and acquaintances. There was also a small article about the car that had been abandoned on old River Road, along with a picture of the missing owner.

When all the news and coffee had been consumed, Reddick pulled out Freddie's file. He called the numbers available for his contacts again, and again no one had seen or heard from him. He left a message with each contact to have Freddie call his office if they heard from him. He was not going to hold his breath on this one, but for now, it was the best he could do.

It was clear this was going to be a waiting game. There was nothing to do at this point but to dive back into the "tomorrow basket" and stay close to the phone. At this rate, he would have to be careful or he might work himself out of a job!

****

When Reddick looked up at the clock, the day was nearly over. He had not heard from the Chief today... maybe there was nothing new to report. Reddick hoped that no news was good news, but deep down he knew everyone was just waiting for the other shoe to drop. In reality, it had been too long for this thing to turn out good... now it was just a matter of waiting.

He decided against calling the Chief. He knew he was busy with this situation and would call him if there were any changes.

With that decision made, Reddick got his jacket and put the newspaper in his pocket; he knew Bruce would be interested in the articles. He walked down the hall and signaled to Elsie that he was leaving. She looked up at him and gave him a knowing smile as she nodded. He knew immediately he had messed up and given her the wrong idea. Setting a precedent for turning out this much work was not a smart thing to do, as he could easily ruin a reputation that had taken him years to build. He had no intention of working this hard on a regular basis.

****

Reddick had just walked in from the garage when the phone rang. Penny answered and gave him a questioning look.

"It's the Chief," she said, with her hand over the mouthpiece. She slowly handed him the receiver.

Reddick greeted the Chief and then was silent for what seemed to be an eternity. After a few "yeses" and "I sees," he thanked the Chief and hung up the phone.

Penny and Bruce knew the Chief was updating Reddick on the events of the day. They stood there waiting, looking at him with an air of expectation... they wanted to know every detail, too.

"According to the Chief, today they found the right car... the car belonging to Stevens. They found it less than a quarter mile from the Stevens' house. He said they had reports the car had been there for at least two days, maybe longer. Now there's little doubt that foul play is a factor. He said they were going over the car and dusting for prints at this very moment and he feels sure they'll come up with some kind of new evidence or lead in this thing." As Reddick said this, every nerve in his body seemed to tense. It took him vocalizing what the Chief had said to actually realize the severity and implications of his statements.

Almost in a trance, Reddick pulled the <u>Tribune</u> from his jacket pocket and handed it to Bruce. He then walked back into the kitchen to get a glass of tea. Was all this really happening? The weather had not broken all week; maybe it was his imagination and this could be the symptoms of a heat stroke. One sip of the cold tea and Reddick knew he was awake and was sure as hell not dreaming.

When he went back into the living room, he saw that Bruce had slumped on the sofa and was deep into the articles. When his eyes met with the picture of the missing woman, he froze. The color drained from his face and he stammered as he began to tell his brother about the connection.

"This woman was with Gillespie! She attended the parties and took the pictures... I know she must be involved in all this!" Bruce tried to contain his excitement as he told Reddick as much as he could remember about the woman.

This was mind-blowing news. He had to think about this. In the back of his mind, he was not at all sure that he wanted to share this new information with anyone... not just yet anyway. Reddick convinced Bruce to just keep a lid on this until he got the chance to talk face-to-face with the Chief.

****

Reddick had gotten into the office a little later than usual. After his conversation with the Chief last night and the tantalizing information from Bruce, he could not remember closing his eyes all night. A million questions kept running through his mind. Is it possible after Sandra found the pictures, Bruce simply lost it, and did something irrational and stupid? On the other hand, where in the hell is Freddie? Maybe he and his friend made contact and things got out of hand. I can't find him, so how in the hell am I supposed to know what's going on?

The complexity of the situation and the sketchy information was making this puzzle hard to put together. Did the pieces fit, and if so, how? There had to be some way to make sense of it.

Since Elsie was busy processing all the work Reddick had been turning out the last couple of days, he poured his own coffee and picked up the paper on his way back to his desk.

He sat down and moved a stack of folders so he could spread out the paper. The Thursday <u>Tribune</u> headline was sensational, to say the very least!

"Car Found Abandoned - Foul Play Suspected!"

The article went on to describe where and when the car was found and by whom. Of course it did not say whether any evidence had been found. It only said the car was being processed and dusted for fingerprints. It did, however, rehash previous articles and information from friends and family, some of which had been printed the day before.

All this was old news to Reddick. After scanning through all the articles, he picked up the phone.

"Hi, Mom. How is Dad feeling today?" Reddick asked.

"He's been worried to death, Reddick. He's called Bruce several times and Sandra won't call him to the phone or give him a message. I just don't know what's going on with that girl. You know, I think she just does things to try to upset your father."

"Now, Mom, you know Sandra's having a hard time right now. It's almost time for the baby and this heat has to be very hard on her."

"Well, I guess you're right, but your father would rest easier if Bruce would come by for a few minutes or at least give him a call."

"Tell Dad I called and that I'll see to it Bruce gives him a call. Love you, Mom... talk to you later." With that, his obligatory call to his parents had been made... he felt he was a *good* son.

Reddick grabbed his jacket and his briefcase and rushed out the front door. He had Court this morning and the Judge was still pissed at him for being late last time. He had no sooner cleared the door to the courtroom, than the solicitor called him over to his table.

"Reddick, I'm going to have to postpone this again. I hope it won't be a problem for you. I just need a little more time."

"No problem for me. As soon as you get it on the calendar, let me know," Reddick responded.

With that, he left the courtroom and went down the stairs to the Record Room... the room in the courthouse commonly known as the "information room." It houses all the old documents that have officially been recorded for the County, but more importantly, it's the center to acquire any new undocumented information, such as any rumors that may be currently circulating.

After spending an hour or two in the record room talking first to one friend and then another, he ran into R. D., one of the businessmen from the Beacon Club. They briefly discussed the current rumors, and then R. D. asked if Reddick had time for lunch.

After they left the Courthouse, his friend asked the second question. This one was more under his breath, "Reddick, did you have anything to do with this missing persons thing?"

Reddick's immediate answer was, "Of course not!"

Over lunch, R.D. stated he had the usual concerns about the situation, but he also made the statement that "we," meaning the club members, may not have to do anything about this problem after all... it looked as though someone else may well have taken care of it for us. There was absolutely no remorse in his tone.

He wanted to know if a time had been set for another meeting. Reddick told him it would have to wait until this missing persons thing was cleared up. The Chief seemed to be on it 24-7 right now.

They hurriedly finished up their lunch and returned to their respective offices.

Reddick was sick of work, sick of the unrelenting heat and most of all sick of waiting. Thursday afternoon was nothing but a torment.

The Chief had called while he was at lunch and left a message that nothing new had turned up. Reddick still had heard nothing from Freddie. And the queers were still missing.

Reddick had given up on any resolution for the day, so he called home. After the pleasantries, he asked Penny if he could speak to Bruce.

"Hey, what's going on?" was Bruce's greeting.

"Hey, you sound a little better than you have in a few days," Reddick answered. "I talked to Mom this morning. She said Dad was feeling pretty low. How about I pick you up and we drop by there for a few minutes this afternoon? I really think it would mean a lot to the Old Man."

"If you think we have to, sure, why not? Guess I might as well get this over with sooner rather than later," Bruce said with dread in his voice.

"No, No, Bruce. You have the wrong idea. We're not going over there to share our problems. We're going over there to see how they are - and let them see we're still alive. Put your brave face on and I'll pick you up in 20 minutes," Reddick said and hung up the phone.

He scooped up the paper and his jacket and was out the door giving Elsie a faint wave as he passed her desk. She knew she had seen the last of him, at least for the rest of the day.

****

Reddick remembered he had an early appointment on Friday. Frankly, had it not been for that one thing, he probably would not have gone into the office at all. Fridays were always the slowest day of the week. Since there was no Court, there was almost no business. Most of the law offices in town didn't even bother to open. He had thought about discussing a scheduling change with Elsie, and maybe, someday, he would be brave enough to do just that. He chuckled to himself. She had been with the firm longer than he had and had been his father's right arm for many years. With any luck at all, she would still be there for many more. Elsie was a jewel, but he wasn't about to let her know he was at all fond of her.

Reddick arrived at the office before anyone else. He made a pot of coffee and sat in the break room looking over the paper while the brew perked. There was very little to say today that had not already been said... no new developments, only more speculation. Having seen all he wanted to about the time the coffee quit gurgling, he poured himself a cup and made his way back to his office. He thumbed through a few phone messages from yesterday, but nothing got his attention. He straightened his desk and prepared for his meeting.

****

The meeting turned out to be, by far, the easiest thing he had done all week. A simple dictation and a mid-week filing... a piece of cake!

Reddick had a wild idea and wanted something more challenging to do... so bravely, he picked up the phone and dialed Sandra's number. First he had to persuade her to let him come over to talk. This relationship was at an impasse and someone had to start the communication. After all, Bruce could not stay at his house forever! Once Sandra was willing to listen, then all he had to do was convince Bruce to ask her to forgive him. This is a good plan, he thought. He then spent the majority of the day convincing Sandra to listen to what Bruce had to say.

The day was finally over. At least Bruce and Sandra were being civil and a dialogue had begun. Bruce had not started drinking again, but he *was* still staying with Reddick and Penny. Three out of four's not all bad.

At dinner, Reddick realized he had not heard from the Chief all day. He quickly surmised there was nothing new or he would have already called. Reddick decided to settle back for a quiet night at home with the television and the window fan.

What a week, he thought to himself. What a friggin' week!

Bruce seemed to be doing remarkably well considering all the turmoil and anxiety the past week had delivered. He seemed to have a certain peace about him that, frankly, bothered Reddick more than he cared to admit.

Even tonight, Bruce had decided to turn in early. He politely excused himself right after dinner and retired to the spare bedroom. At first, Reddick thought maybe he just wanted to give him and Penny a chance to spend some time together... three is generally considered a crowd. Then the old uncertainty of "why" kept coming back to mind. It wasn't Bruce's nature to be that considerate, and that in itself concerned Reddick.

A few hours later the phone rang. A chill ran over Reddick when he reached for the receiver. Before he could even say hello, he heard the Chief's voice and a lot of noise in the background.

"They found'em, Reddick, they found 'em... They said it was a massacre!" the Chief exclaimed, almost out of breath. **"Come to the office and go down there with us."**

"I'm on my way," Reddick replied as he slipped his shoes on and grabbed his keys.

He looked over at Penny with fear in his eyes. "The Chief just called to say they've found them!"

"Where are they?"

"He didn't say, he just said - *it's bad*!"

"Oh, my God," she murmured, putting her hands over her mouth.

"He asked me to ride with 'em to the scene. I don't know how long it'll take; but I'll be back as soon as I can."

"Aren't you going to tell Bruce?"

"No, don't wake him... he's had enough excitement this week. I'll fill him in when I find out what's going on."

Reddick kissed Penny on the forehead and hurried toward the door.

"Be careful!" she called after him.

No one in the Munroe household slept on Friday night, except for Bruce.

Discovery.........

By the time Reddick got downtown, the Chief was already in his car and had a couple of VIPs with him. The group consisted of a detective and a couple guys from the Beacon Club. The Chief was in the driver seat and his lead detective was up front with him. He was on the radio trying to get directions and confirm the exact location. Bo and R.D. were in the back seat. "Room for one more?" Reddick asked, as he climbed in with them.

As they turned down Main Street, everyone was asking questions at the same time. Finally the Chief said, "Alright now, listen up! This is what I know so far. Bud from over at the Sheriff's Office called an hour ago to tell me they think they may have located my missing persons. He said late this afternoon a couple of men who work at Lake Summit called in to the Station to report finding some bodies. They were dumping a load of brush up next to the dam when they stumbled on 'em. They claimed to have found three victims. From what he understood, the bodies were in pretty bad shape... they must have been there for a while. The deputies found a wallet and were able to ID Stevens. They're not sure, but suspect the other male to be Gillespie. He said the bodies were so decomposed it was really hard to tell. He told me the third victim is female... at this time, they don't know who the hell she is!"

By this time, the cruiser was speeding down Highway 176 at a pretty good clip. After slowing for a few sharp curves, the Chief made a sweeping right turn onto a dirt road. After a short distance, he slowed again when he came upon a deputy standing in the middle of the road with a flashlight. The deputy immediately recognized the Chief and waved the car on through. As the car slowed, the deputy directed the Chief to turn left down a narrow lane into what seemed to be total darkness. A few hundred yards further and the darkness opened into a partially lighted field.

The Chief pulled his cruiser in beside one of the Sheriff's deputies who was parked away from the activity. As he got out, he took the keys from the ignition before closing his door. He went around and unlocked the trunk and took out a box containing half a dozen flashlights. He said, "I know you boys didn't bring one, so make sure I get these back." With that, he turned from the group and walked the short distance to witness this horrifying tragedy for himself.

The officers on the scene were trying their best to use car headlights and flashlights to illuminate the area.

The authorities, as well as the civilian onlookers were in a trance-like state... the gruesome site was surreal. The atmosphere more closely resembled that of a circus, rather than a crime scene. This turn of events was a very unexpected climax to their weeklong search.

As the news spread, officers and curious onlookers were continuously arriving from all the nearby counties. They were everywhere. People were just gawking, milling around and between the bodies. The untrained observers handled objects that had been placed on and around the victims as if they could single-handedly solve the mystery by just touching and rearranging every object at the scene. Should there have been any salvageable evidence, the uncontrolled crowd had methodically destroyed it.

After speaking with Ben from the Sheriff's Office, Reddick learned that the Sheriff himself was yet to arrive on the scene. This, Reddick thought to be a little strange, since everyone else in the three county area had already arrived. It was very clear whose jurisdiction this was, as far as the investigation was concerned. Maybe this was the reason there was so much chaos and confusion. The "ringleader" was not there to direct the show.

Reddick fiddled with his flashlight and finally got the thing to work. He slowly walked over to the area where the bodies were. The smell was so foul it was difficult to get too close and stay there for any extended length of time.

He placed his handkerchief over his nose and mouth and viewed the bodies as thoroughly as possible. He tried to commit to memory every detail, as if his future might depend on his ability to recall some minor item. Almost immediately he sensed something was just "not right" about what he saw. Although he wasn't a trained inves-tigator, several things about the way the bodies were left troubled him.

He happened to be standing close to Bud as he was questioning one of the men who had discovered the bod-ies earlier in the evening. As he listened, Reddick quickly picked up on the fact that Stevens' body was face down when they found him. "The back of his head and neck looked black," the man explained to the officer. "I just turned the body over to see if it was a Negro. When I saw he was white, we didn't touch anything else, we just went up the road to call for help."

As Reddick watched, Bud then stooped between the bodies of the male victims. As he observed them, he could not help but notice that Stevens, although his skull had been crushed, looked relatively neat for the length of time he had been there.

Gillespie, on the other hand, in addition to a crushed skull, had blood all over the front of his shirt. Taking a closer look, Bud noticed the unusual puncture marks on his chest and numerous wounds of the same type on his neck.

His crutches had been laid across his body in a strange, maybe ritualistic manner.

Reddick then turned and slowly walked over to the body of the female victim. It was horrifying how she was brutalized. He immediately noticed that she had suffered the identical puncture wounds as Gillespie. It was evident she had been killed with a fatal blow to the head, as were the first two victims. As he looked at the items around the corpse, he did notice something very strange about the way she was undressed. The bra was lying down next to the right leg, but how was it possible for the blouse to be around both arms and the bra to be off? The blouse would have had to be completely off both arms before the bra could have been removed. Was Reddick the only one to notice such a critical detail?

From what he saw, there was a fair amount of blood around the heads of the victims, but Reddick was convinced this field was not the scene of the crime!

After several hours of observing the horrific atrocity of the so-called crime scene investigation, Reddick and the others climbed back into the Chief's car and headed back to town.

The Chief briefly broke the silence of the passengers during the ride back. "Well, looks like we have a hell-of-a-mess on our hands, boys." The mood was somber; no one seemed to want to comment further. The impact of the gruesome sight had taken its toll, but it was the overwhelming odor that had sickened everyone. The unseasonable heat and humidity, even at this hour of the evening, had contributed to the overpowering feeling of nauseousness and suffocation. It was unlike anything anyone in the group had ever smelled before. A few spectators at the scene had even vomited due to the gore and horrible stench. This experience would not be quickly forgotten.

Reddick's mind was racing as he quietly sat pressed between the two big guys in the back seat. He guessed the Chief would have more than a few questions needing immediate answers once they got back to the Station.

As they neared the downtown area, the streetlights provided a flickering glimpse inside the vehicle. As they got closer to the Station, Reddick glanced up into the Chief's rearview mirror. At that split second, his eyes met the Chief's. With this glance, each man knew a meeting was going to take place as soon as the Chief could rid himself of this audience. This could prove to be a very long night.

The Chief pulled the cruiser into the reserved parking space at the front of the Station. Everyone lethargically rolled out of the cruiser and into the office. A couple of the guys headed straight for the men's room. The others either went directly to the Chief's office or to a vacant desk to use the phone. The Chief rounded the corner of his desk and slid into his chair. He quickly reached for the small stack of phone messages that had come in while he had been gone... nothing looked so important it couldn't wait until morning.

After a few minutes, everyone converged around the desk in the Chief's office. During what seemed to be hours of discussion, no one mentioned having noticed the glaring inconsistencies at the crime scene. It seemed to be the consensus that the victims were murdered where they were found. Reddick could not remember who first mentioned this was probably a cult killing, but it quickly caught on. If the investigators were not able to come up with a better motive or pull a rabbit out of a hat after the destruction of the crime scene, they may attribute this whole thing to Voodoo.

The excitement of rehashing the activity at the crime scene was slowly giving way to the exhaustion everyone felt after such a stressful evening. Finally, one of the guys happened to notice the time and the group started to break up.

It was well after midnight before the last of the men bid his goodnight leaving Reddick sitting across the desk from the Chief. After giving his investigator sufficient time to clear the building, the Chief rose and walked around Reddick to securely close and lock the office door. He then returned to his chair, lighting another cigarette.

For what seemed to be an eternity, neither man said a word. They just stared into emptiness, neither knowing how or where to start what could be a very sensitive conversation.

Finally the Chief broke the silence. "Reddick, tell me again you had nothing to do with this. Tell me you know nothing at all about it."

"Chief, you know me better than that - you've been my father's friend and friend to my family for as long as I can remember..."

"Don't beat around the bush, Reddick – just answer the damn question!" the Chief exploded.

" *I give you my word, Chief... I had nothing to do with this,*" Reddick replied. In his heart he was praying to God that Bruce or Freddie didn't have anything to do with it either.

"You realize, based on what you told me last Friday morning, I have to call Bruce in for questioning. Due to what I know at this time, your brother Bruce is the prime suspect in this, Reddick," the Chief said as he looked directly at him.

"You know Bruce couldn't have done this! Sure, he was plenty upset about the pictures, but *surely you know he couldn't have done something like this.*"

As Reddick heard his own words, he wondered if he was trying to convince the Chief or convince himself. With that, a flush of color came to Reddick's face. As a distraction, he quickly pulled out his handkerchief and pretended to catch a sneeze. He couldn't allow a brief moment of sensitivity to be mistaken for guilt.

"Bruce is staying at my house," Reddick stated as he put away his handkerchief. "Let me bring him in tomorrow. I know once you talk to him, you'll be satisfied he had nothing to do with this. Let's not jump the gun on this, Chief. You know to officially bring him in would set this town on fire. It would be a public scandal... not to mention what that would do to the Old Man."

"Okay, okay, bring Bruce in here at 11:00 tomorrow morning. I won't consider it official. There'll be no record of the interview, and if I feel you're right in what you're telling me, there'll be no record of him being a suspect at all. Agreed?"

"I'll have him here at 11:00 sharp," Reddick firmly stated as he rose from his chair.

The Chief said nothing as he walked around the desk to unlock the door.

Both men seemed to meet at the door with outstretched hands. The Chief firmly grasped Reddick's hand. This hand shake between gentlemen was confirmation of trust and a sign of mutual respect.

Reddick was out the door and half way home before he realized a sense of place.

Aftermath ....

Reddick had not closed his eyes all night. The images of the crime scene and the horrible "stench of the place" seemed to be engraved in his memory. The only thing that could possibly overshadow that nightmare was his later conversation with the Chief. The fact he may still have a few doubts about the innocence of Bruce or himself was more terrifying to Reddick than the actual discovery of the bodies.

He realized this situation put the Chief in a very awkward and precarious position. Knowing him to be an honorable man, the Chief would have already hauled in the entire Munroe family if necessary, were it not for the Old Man.

The newspaper hit the front porch with a thud at about 4:30 a.m. The sound broke Reddick's wide-eyed concentration on the ceiling, but he continued to just lie there, rerunning the details of this enormously complex chain of events over in his mind as though it was a horror film.

Knowing that Penny had slept little after his late night description of the gruesome discovery, he knew she needed
a couple more hours of rest before tackling what was sure
to be another stressful day.

Reddick sluggishly rolled over and slid out of bed, trying not to wake her. He quietly closed the bedroom door
and made his way down the hall to the kitchen. After putting on a pot of coffee, he then headed to the front door
to get the paper... it was surprisingly large for a Saturday
morning edition.

Walking back to the kitchen, he paused in front of the
large mirror in the hallway. His reflection revealed a much
older man than it had even a couple of weeks ago. Taking
a closer look at his eyes, he was surprised to see how swol-
len they actually were. For the last few days they had
been hurting, but they now looked as if they might begin
to bleed at any moment.

He continued to the kitchen and started to open the
paper as he sat down at the table. When he took a look at
the headlines, he immediately put his personal discomfort
aside.

His aching eyes were glued to the print. He felt numb
as he read about the horror, line-by-line. The bold black
and white of the print verified that he had, indeed, seen
what he thought he had seen. The events, as they unfolded last night, were real. He had been there. This whole
thing could have so easily been a bad dream. For some

unknown reason, Reddick had an awful gut feeling that the bad dream was just beginning.

As he was connecting his own memories of the crime scene to the graphic photographs in the paper, Bruce ambled into the kitchen. He walked past Reddick and reached into the cabinet for a coffee mug. "Want a cup?" he asked as he poured the hot brew into the first mug.

"Yeah," Reddick replied, as he moved some of the papers out of the way so Bruce could sit down.

"What's all this?" Bruce questioned, as he took a chair across the table from his brother.

Reddick reluctantly pushed the print over in front of Bruce. "Son-of-a-Bitch!" Bruce exclaimed, as he looked over at Reddick accusingly. *"Is this how you fix things... you had this done?"*

"Of course I didn't!" Reddick flashed back.

"But you told me you had taken care of it! You said not to worry about it, it was over!" Bruce was getting louder and louder.

Reddick then told Bruce about his meeting on Friday morning at the Club. He told him how he had explained the delicate problem, and the members had agreed to give the matter consideration over the weekend and get back together on Monday. He told Bruce he was confident they could come up with a resolution and get this thing taken care of diplomatically.

"I was just trying to take the edge off... I felt with the guys' help, we could resolve this thing. We just needed a little time," Reddick continued.

Bruce seemed to relax a little after hearing what seemed to be a logical enough explanation. Even though Bruce was not a member of the Club, he certainly knew everything about it. His father had started it many years ago with the purpose of gently and silently regulating the growth and direction of the town. These members continued to share and shoulder that responsibility. Bruce had, from time-to-time, felt a little jealous and maybe even slighted because he had not yet been invited to join.

Reddick then began to relate in detail the events of the past evening to Bruce in detail.

"There **is** just one thing," Reddick hesitantly continued. "Because of what I told the guys Friday morning, the Chief says you may be considered a suspect in this."

"Suspect... what the hell are you talking about?" Bruce retorted.

"Now, just listen a minute before you get too excited," Reddick came back. "Since he thinks you have a strong motive, he wants to talk to you at the Station at 11:00 this morning. He just wants to know where you were and verify for himself you're not involved. *Don't worry*, he said this would be unofficial."

"Well, we know there won't be a problem," Bruce replied confidently. "Jimmy can vouch for my whereabouts.

I never thought that being laid up drunk would ever be a good thing, but I guess it'll save my ass this time."

****

At 10:50 a.m. on Saturday, July 23, Reddick and Bruce walked up the steps and into the front door of the Police Station. Normally, on Saturday mornings, this place would be running on a skeleton crew; however, the magnitude of last night's discovery had transformed it into a beehive of activity. They spoke casually with several of the officers as they made their way down the hall... after all, they knew everyone at the Station and no one there knew the purpose of the visit, other than the Chief. Bruce and Reddick tried to play down their anxiety and act as normally as possible.

When Reddick opened the door, the Chief was sitting behind his desk talking on the phone. There were three officers standing in front of him. When the Chief looked up and acknowledged their presence, he abruptly ended his conversation. He spoke briefly with the detectives, giving each a list of people to find and interview. They were soon on their way and the office was cleared.

The Chief then motioned the Munroe brothers to take a seat. He lifted the telephone receiver and punched in a couple of numbers. "Harold, please come back here and tell Lois we aren't to be disturbed."

After a few minutes Harold entered the office and the Chief motioned for him to close the door. From the look on his face, Reddick knew that Harold didn't know what this was all about. The Chief looked directly at Harold and told him the interrogation that was about to take place was not to leave his office. Harold, being his most trusted and loyal officer, immediately knew exactly what the Chief meant.

Harold sat down on the corner of a small filing cabinet. The Chief looked over at Bruce. "Now, tell me about your weekend."

Bruce looked at Reddick and then back to the Chief. "I guess you know about the pictures," Bruce began.

"Yes, Reddick briefly described your precarious situation last Friday morning," the Chief replied.

"Well, Reddick told me he would see what he could do. He told me to go home and to *be cool* until he got back to me. My wife Sandra raised hell at me because I was out all night Thursday night, but she can verify that I was at home sleeping off a drunk most of the day Friday. I thought this whole thing was over when Reddick called me Saturday morning. He said he had taken care of it," Bruce continued.

The immediate glare Reddick got from the Chief almost made his heart stop. The Chief quickly looked back as Bruce continued, "I'm sure Sandra suspected something was wrong. While I was sleeping, she went through my briefcase. When she found the pictures, she went ballistic! She totally lost it... she flew into a rage and threw me out."

The Chief again looked hard at Reddick, "What time was this?"

"I think it was around 10:30 or 11:00."

"Then what did you do?"

"Well... I went down to the Blackbird. I needed a drink... maybe a lot of drinks after that."

"How long did you stay there?" the Chief asked as he repositioned himself in his chair.

"I don't exactly remember what time it was, but I was there 'till Reddick picked me up on Monday."

The Chief nodded at Harold. He got up and quietly left the room.

The Chief made small talk while Harold was gone. He made light of Bruce having been thrown out, as if it was a 'right of passage' for every married man.

After a few minutes, Harold came back into the room and nodded to the Chief. It was understood Harold had simply and quickly verified Bruce's alibi. The Chief had known Jimmy and his family forever... if Jimmy said Bruce was with him, then Bruce was with him.

There were a few more minutes of small talk. The Chief thanked Bruce for coming in and asked him not to leave town in case he had more questions for him. As Bruce and Reddick rose to go, the Chief said, "Reddick, I have a few questions for you, if you don't mind."

Reddick's face quickly flushed. He knew what was coming. "Sure, Chief," he said as he sat back down.

"Harold, show Bruce back up front and buy him a coke. We'll be right behind you," the Chief said.

Harold and Bruce went out the door, securely closing it as they left. The Chief looked over at Reddick with an expression of anger on his face.

"Don't bullshit me, Reddick." he exploded. "You took care of it? **You took care of it?** Exactly how the hell did you take care of it?" the Chief exclaimed.

"I didn't do anything. I just told him that so he would quit drinking... that's all. I knew if he thought it was over, the chances were better he would stay sober. I figured "we" would soon decide how to take care of the problem. I was just buying time, that's all, Chief, I swear!"

"Reddick, don't think you can play me! You had better be leveling with me, or so help me, even **your father** won't be able to save your ass!"

With that, the Chief went around his desk and opened the door. The minute they walked through that door, everything was completely normal again. No one outside that office would have ever guessed there had been such an exchange.

Once up front, the Chief acted as though the Munroe brothers' visit was of a social nature.

"I'll give you a call when we get some feedback from the Sheriff's Department," the Chief said as he shook Reddick's hand.

Reddick and Bruce went out the door and down the steps.

"Everything all right?" Bruce questioned Reddick as they walked back to the car.

"Sure, everything is fine," Reddick replied, expressing a sigh of relief.

****

The Chief retreated to his office. He reached for the phone as he seated himself behind the desk. After quickly dialing a familiar number, he asked, "Is Ben around?"

"Just a minute," was the reply from the deputy answering the switchboard.

The Chief was thinking how he could at least keep his foot in the door where this investigation was concerned. He knew full well the Sheriff's Department was in control, but he needed to keep a finger on the pulse of this thing just in case Reddick was involved and the whole thing went south.

In a few minutes Ben was on the line.

"Ben, has anyone been sent out to Clarence Gillespie's house yet?" the Chief questioned.

"No, we haven't dispatched anyone out there yet," Ben immediately replied, recognizing the Chief's voice. "I'm taking a deputy and going out there myself in half an hour."

"Would you mind a little company?" the Chief then asked.

"We'll meet you out there in 30 minutes," Ben replied as he replaced the receiver.

The Chief had known Ben since childhood. They hadn't been that close growing up, but in the last five or six years their paths had regularly crossed due to their work. They each respected and admired the other. In past years, they both had been recognized for their dedication and professionalism in law enforcement.

****

Since Reddick and Bruce had not eaten breakfast, they decided to grab an early lunch. The Home Food Shop on Main Street usually had a good selection of real food, so they chose that over a donut from the bakery. The café was usually crowded on Saturdays and today was no exception. It seemed everyone had seen the paper or heard the rumors about the murders. There were few strangers in this local diner, so everyone there freely discussed what they had heard or read. It seemed everyone had an opinion on what had happened, even though few knew any of the details.

Half way through the meal, Bruce looked across the table at Reddick. "Where would you guess the pictures are?" he asked in a lowered voice. "You don't think someone did this to get them, do you?"

"That's a good possibility," Reddick replied. "If they were trying to blackmail you, they probably had other targets, too. Maybe they tried to blackmail the wrong person."

"Did you tell the Chief I knew who the woman was and she was connected to Stevens and Gillespie?"

"No. I'm sure in time they'll figure it out. This whole situation is pretty hot right now... we don't need any more involvement until we can figure out where the pictures are. Let's just let our comrades feed us information until we get a handle on this," Reddick stated almost sinisterly.

With this statement, Bruce was taken aback. He had never heard this tone from his brother. Was there some hidden meaning he was not aware of? This realization only made Bruce again question whether his brother was somehow involved, and if so, to what extent. For the first time in his life, Bruce felt a measure of responsibility. He was beginning to realize how grave the consequences could be in this matter... he grew quiet; he was really starting to feel guilty now. What had he made of his brother... or more importantly, what had his brother done to protect him? This whole affair seemed to be his fault. If he hadn't been so arrogant and stupid, he wouldn't be in this mess. Getting mixed up in this would certainly destroy his reputation and that of every member of his family. Most likely he had already ruined his marriage and the rest of his life for that matter. What would the Old Man think... this would probably destroy him.

The waitress refilling their tea glasses broke his negative concentration and brought Bruce back to the present.

They quickly finished up lunch and agreed to go by the office for a few minutes. Reddick went directly down the hall and into his office. He hung his jacket across the back of a chair as he gently pushed the door almost closed. As he collapsed into his leather chair, he reached for the pile of legal folders on the top of his desk. Quickly flipping through them, he came to the one labeled "Frederick Johnson."

This seemed to be a repetition of what he'd done so many times before. He dialed all the same reference numbers, talked to all the same people and they said the same thing they had the last time he'd called. Freddie seemed to have fallen off the face of the earth.

Was it possible, Reddick thought to himself, that Freddie and his slimy friend could have killed these three and then disappeared into the woodwork? He was beginning to question his confidence in what Freddie might divulge if the authorities ever did catch up to him. These were not pleasant thoughts.

Reddick opened his desk drawer and pulled out a telephone directory. He quickly looked up the number for Vincent Stevens and scribbled down the address. It seemed familiar and he felt reasonably sure he could find it. Next, he did the same for Clarence Gillespie. His address was not at all familiar... Reddick had to pull the city map out for this one. After noting the general location, he quickly wrote down the address and tore the page from his legal pad.

Reddick started back down the hall and as he stopped at Bruce's door, he could tell that he was on the phone with Sandra. He stuck up his index finger to let Reddick know that he would be with him in a minute, and then promptly finished his conversation. They soon left the office and were back in the car headed out Fifth Avenue toward Laurel Park.

"So, how's it going with Sandra?" Reddick asked as he looked over at Bruce.

"At least we're talking... I guess that's a start. Where're we going?" Bruce asked as they crossed Church Street and he put on his sunglasses.

"I thought we would take a ride by Gillespie's house and see if we can learn anything," Reddick said as he too put on his glasses.

Reddick turned to the right off Fifth Avenue one street too soon. As soon as he realized what he'd done, he started looking to his left, hoping that he'd be able to see into the backyard at Gillespie's house. "This is a lot more wooded than I thought it would be," he said as he was maneuvering his new car up the narrow lane. "I'll just go around the block and hopefully we'll be able to take a good look."

"What exactly are we looking for?" Bruce questioned as he craned his neck to see what Reddick was so interested in.

"With any luck at all, an officer from one of the divisions will be here. If we're even luckier, it'll be somebody we know who can get us inside to look around. We *are* still looking for those pictures, right?"

"You don't miss a beat, do you?"

As they slowly cruised back down Broadway, they saw what they had hoped for. A County car was parked in the drive beside the Chief's cruiser. They slowly pulled up into the drive and parked behind the cars.

Reddick called out as he opened the front door. The Chief called back at him from the kitchen, "Come on in boys, but don't touch anything." As they made their way in, the Chief continued, "The lab boys haven't gotten here to process anything yet. From the looks of it, there may be damn little to process."

Just as they got into the kitchen, Ben called in to the Chief, "You'd better come on out here and see this."

The trio walked out the back door that opened onto a carport. On the south side was a storage room, probably used for a laundry room.

"Someone cut the lock off," Ben said as the trio walked up to the open door. "Looks like this may have been used as a darkroom. Whatever was in here must have been real important to somebody."

They looked inside the small room to find only a make-shift clothesline with some pins on it. Below that, on a small table they saw a few large brown bottles containing some sort of liquid. There beside the bottles were a couple of long, flat pans that could have been used in developing pictures.

Reddick then realized they had at least learned where the developing had taken place... they just didn't know who might have wanted the pictures more than they did. The disappointment showed on Reddick's face as he and Bruce exchanged glances.

There was little reason to hang around any longer. For a lack of anything else to say, Reddick turned to the Chief, "Did you get positive ID on the bodies yet, Chief?"

"Yeah, it was Stevens and Gillespie all right. The woman was from Ashton. The car found last Monday on old River Road belonged to her. We haven't figured out how she fits into this yet, but we will," he replied.

"Guess we had better get out of the way so you guys can do your job," Reddick stated as he and Bruce headed back around the house.

"I'll talk to you later, fellas," the Chief called after them.

During their ride back to Main Street, Reddick realized how odd their unexpected arrival at Gillespie's house might have appeared to the Chief. Though he said nothing, Reddick was sure the Chief understood why they had come. He felt sure he and the Chief had the same idea about the pictures and they both were headed down the same path toward finding them, if possible. Though disappointing, at least one of their questions had been answered, Reddick thought. They had found where the developing had taken place, but someone had beaten them to the goods. He wondered if the blackmail photos could have been the only reason for the murders. It was now evident this complicated situation had suffered yet another baffling twist.

Official Investigation ....

After the discovery of the bodies, everyone who had been interviewed when the search had first begun was re-interviewed. Every comment made by the witnesses and all observations made by the investigators would be re-evaluated and considered in a far more serious light. The slightest detail would be more closely scrutinized.

The organization of the official investigation was very similar to that of the crime scene - chaos and confusion. There were many different departments, and each seemed to be conducting their own independent investigation. Folks were starting to complain they were being interviewed over and over again, first by one agency and then another.

An initial look at the friends and relatives of each of the victims was routine. During the course of these interviews, investigators collected information and clues that led them into an ever-deepening mystery concerning the boisterous parties, illegal drugs and unconventional sex.

The discovery of these types of activities even existing in small town America, frankly shocked most of the local investigators.

Research into the activities of each of the victims on the last day they were seen alive was one of the first orders of business by each of the agencies. That reconstruction would at least give the investigators a time line to work with. A few weeks into the investigation, the assorted agencies began to realize that compilation and sharing of all information gathered would be to the benefit of everyone concerned. These agencies also realized this investigation was going to be far more expensive, not only budget wise, but also in man-hours, than most could afford to do on their own. For this, and coordination reasons, the State Bureau of Investigation began to take the lead and set up a temporary command post. The officers working this station were receiving an overwhelming number of calls and some pretty unbelievable information, the most credible of which was passed along to the various agencies to be checked out. This process had become a daunting task.

As the leads by the various agencies and divisions were being followed up, each agency would inform the others of their progress in report form. Some of the more interesting or unusual reports would be preceded by a phone call giving them a heads-up that the report would be forthcoming.

Part 1 ....

Many of the reports were routine and of little conse-
quence. However, when a report from the neighboring
Bascomb County crossed the desk of the Chief, he immediately called Reddick to come over and read the bizarre
collection of interviews from family and acquaintances of
the female victim.

Reddick had stopped by the bakery on his way to see
the Chief. Since the Chief had gone out of his way to
keep the information flowing in his direction, he thought
he could at least treat him to a fresh cup of coffee and a
pastry.

As Reddick entered the Chief's office, a couple of officers were finishing a conversation with him. As they
passed Reddick in the doorway with a small folder, he
overheard them tell the Chief they would get right on it.
He suspected the Chief had given them some assignment
relative to the ongoing investigation.

"Sit down, Reddick," the Chief said as he looked up and recognized the bakery bag. He broke into a big smile as he opened the bag before him. "It was nice of you to bring the sweets... they could help make this bizarre report more palatable."

The two began to take the lids off the coffee and dig into the bag in search of napkins to contain the sticky, gooey, heavenly treats.

Reddick looked across to see a small folder placed in the center of the desk, presumably from the Bascomb County Sheriff's office. "So the woman has turned out to be a mystery," he said, in more of a statement than a question.

"The boys over there didn't know what to make of it. When they started working on the list of friends and relatives of that woman, they thought it would be pretty much routine. But when they talked to the very first person at the apartment building where she had been living for several years, they immediately knew there would be nothing routine about this. Instead of getting any answers, they only got a lot more questions. What the boys found out just didn't make much sense."

"Take a look at the statement the lady from the apartment building made," the Chief said as he slid a couple of the pages out of the folder and handed them across to Reddick.

Reddick sat his coffee down on the corner of the desk. As he held his sticky pastry in one hand, he took the sheets with the other.

At the top of the page was the name of the officer and the time and date of the interview. After the initial questions concerning the identity and relationship of the person being questioned, the following statement appeared:

"Miss Davis sometimes made and received calls here in my apartment," Mrs. Cole stated. "Understand - I did not intentionally listen in, but being in the same room, you couldn't help but notice her conversations were sometimes strange. They seemed to be in some sort of code. Occasionally, I overheard names of strange cities or towns and some kind of number sequences. I wouldn't dream of asking her about it... I didn't want her to think I'd been eavesdropping."

"I always suspected something strange was going on with her, just for the fact she refused to get a telephone of her own. She only came to use mine a couple times a week; this still seemed real peculiar," Mrs. Cole explained. "It wasn't like she couldn't afford to have a phone of her own, after all, rumor was she had a plant job and made real good money."

"I really didn't mind Miss Davis using my phone occasionally, but having to run urgent messages to her that afternoon was asking too much, I just didn't want to get involved," Mrs. Cole added.

The statement ended and a paragraph followed containing general information obtained while conducting the interviews with other residents in the building:

"It was also learned that Miss Davis was rarely at the apartment she had been renting for the past three years. When she was at home, she was seldom seen out of her apartment, except to use the phone of a neighbor. She was suspiciously quiet and kept to herself, appearing to be very shy and was never known to chitchat or socialize. She seldom had any visitors. The only activity the neighbors had seen at all was one visitor who always came very late at night, as regular as clockwork on Sunday and Wednesday at 11:00 p.m. Miss Davis had never mentioned it, and no one had ever seen the visitor close enough to determine if it was a man or a woman, but the hour of the visit was the unusual thing about it."

When Reddick finished reading the reports he looked across the desk and gave the Chief a puzzled glance. "What do you make of this?" he asked as he handed the copy back over the desk.

"Oh, don't get too excited, it gets even more bizarre!" the Chief stated as he took the papers back and handed Reddick a single sheet. "Seems that her co-workers reported to the detectives she was hard to get to know…. she didn't seem to have a winning personality with any of them either. They said that she never participated in any company activities and flatly refused to come to the Christmas party or attend the annual picnic. Though she was generally quiet and kept to herself, she had proven she could also be mean and racist at times. The gate guard had the most interesting information, however troubling it may prove to be," the Chief continued. "He vividly described the last night he saw her."

Reddick looked down at the sheet to see the familiar heading with date, time, interviewing officer, informant and the word "*Statement:*"

"He said he had just made all of the initial security rounds at the beginning of his shift. The shift change was to begin shortly, so he had to be in the gatehouse to check everybody as they came in. He remembered seeing Miss Davis drive into the parking lot in her '62 Fairlane… he remarked she must have thought she had some 'hot' car. He said he thought there was definitely something weird about that woman. It being Thursday, he knew she would stop by the gatehouse to leave *the* package with him. It had become a weekly routine. He said he had told her over and over the package would be okay in her car if she locked it, but she always insisted he keep it in the gatehouse. He claims he never asked her what was in the package... he didn't particularly like her and he wanted no more conversation with her than was absolutely necessary."

Reddick quickly finished reading the sheet and handed it back across the desk.

The Chief placed the sheet back in the folder. "The boys over there were really dumbfounded when they started to talk to her family," he continued. "They could tell right off that these people knew nothing about her daily habits, much less her friends. The boys got the idea the family was a little embarrassed because they couldn't answer the most basic questions... she was as much a mystery to her own family as she was to everyone else. They knew absolutely nothing except what she *wanted* them to know. This was family, and she was like a total stranger to 'em!"

"Guess she was actually that paranoid, or do you guess she was trying to hide something?" Reddick asked. "Either way, this doesn't make it any easier to explain why she was with Stevens and Gillespie or why she was a victim in this."

"Lord only knows," the Chief replied as he tried to wipe the "goo" off his fingers. "I have a bad feeling about this case... no part of it has been straightforward. With the number of officers and expended man-hours on this, something will surely break in the next day or two... I just hope we get a break on it while it's still relatively fresh."

"I agree. Something this bad just can't happen in a small town without somebody knowing something."

"Oh, I feel sure there's somebody out there who knows what happened. It could be they don't have the gumption to know they might have information that could be helpful... or, on the other hand, it could be somebody who doesn't *want* to come forward out of fear. For whatever reason, they may not want to get involved," the Chief thoughtfully said.

"I imagine if they knew too much, they could be too scared to report anything," Reddick said as he got up and started picking up the cups and napkins from the desk.

"You're right, Reddick," the Chief replied. "That's what I'm afraid of... nobody says anything because they're afraid, or they do talk and maybe it gets 'em killed. Until we get this case solved, our lives are gonna' be hell."

Reddick had put the trash back in the bakery bag and put it in the can beside the door. "I really appreciate you letting me read over your shoulder on this, Chief," he said as he opened the door.

"No problem, Reddick, I'll be in touch as information comes in."

"Thanks a lot," Reddick said as he went out the door, gently closing it behind him.

Part 2 ....

Meanwhile, the local detectives were getting more leads and off-the-wall information than they would be able to follow up in a decade! Some of the tips were so farfetched they didn't even bother to make note of them.

Every day or two the Chief would give Reddick a call to update him with any new information.

A few weeks into the investigation, the detectives thought they had sufficient information and leads to name Mike Franks a suspect. When the Chief found out about it, he took a particular interest and called Ben at the Sheriff's Office to ask for a copy of the report – ASAP.

When it arrived, he did a quick scan and immediately picked up the phone. "Reddick, I think you might want to come over here and take a look at this."

"I'll be there in ten minutes," Reddick replied.

The Chief was almost halfway through the report when Reddick took a seat across the desk from him.

"Reddick, seems we may have a break in the investigation. I'm not so sure it concerns the murders as much as it might have to do with the missing photographs," he said as he handed the new report across his desk.

"This statement was taken from someone who knows a close friend of Mike Franks," the Chief continued. "Seems right after the murders, this friend of Mike's got a little too drunk down at the Blackbird Bar and started shooting off his mouth. The stuff he was bragging about doing sure does fit the timeline for the day of the killings. I think the Sheriff's Department has already called this guy in for questioning, but according to Ben, he's denying everything... says he didn't even see Mike that day. They interrogated Franks last week and it appears that he has an airtight alibi. I think I might go down to Charlottesville the first of next week and talk to him myself," he said. "It can't hurt."

Reddick had started to read the report and appeared to be consumed by the print on the page... he had been so anxious to get any kind of break. Weeks had passed since the thing exploded and the only news was there had been no new developments.

Reddick's eyes had scanned down the page so rapidly on the first reading, he was afraid he might have missed a detail. He flipped back to the first page and began to read more slowly and carefully. He wanted to absorb every single word and hoped to pick up any tidbit that might be hiding between the lines.

At the top of the report was the letterhead of the County Sheriff's Department. It stated the date and the time of the interrogation. The deputy's name who took the report was listed next, followed by: "The Following Statements made by Hank Edwards as told to Donald Burtson at the Blackbird Bar on August 5, 1966."

As Reddick started to carefully read the report, in his mind he tried to visualize exactly how this could have taken place.

"Me and Robbie were riding with Mike about 5:30 Sunday. We drove by the Stevens house to the end of the street and turned around. We didn't see nobody on the street... there was nobody out. Mike pulled in the driveway up close to the house. That's when we saw that the front door was standin' open. Mike got out and went to the door and called out. He didn't see nobody and nobody answered him; so he pushed the door all the way open. He didn't hear nothin' so he thought nobody was home. He turned 'round and motioned us to come on in.

We didn't waste no time getting up on the front porch and in the door. Mike told us not to touch nothin' and to follow him in to what he thought was Vince's bedroom. Mike said he'd only been there one other time, and he wasn't that familiar with it. Since Vince lived in the house with his old man, there wasn't no partyin' goin' on there. Mike said

Vince hadn't told his old man he was queer... he sure as hell didn't want him know'n about that.

There was a coat and necktie layin' across the bottom of the bed, but besides that, there wasn't no way to tell if we were even in Vince's room. Mike went to check out the other bedroom, and then called us 'cause he knew that one was Vince's. We followed him in there and checked *everywhere*... the wardrobe, under the bed, and in all the dresser drawers... everywhere. About the time we thought we'd struck out, Robbie stooped down to take a look behind the table by the bed. He saw what looked like the corner of a brown envelope sticking out from under the mattress. He grabbed at it and it ripped, but finally he got it free from the bed coverings.

Mike had a big grin on his face when Robbie handed the envelope to him... thinkin' we had lucked out... then he turned the envelope over to open it and that's when he saw the note scribbled on the front:

> "Here are a couple of the photos you
> asked for. I can make as many copies
> as you want, any time.
>
> Affectionately,
> Clarence

When Mike saw that note, he got *real mad*... he yelled at us to get the hell outta' there. We went out just like we got in... we left the door standin' open just like we found it.

We got back to the car real quick and got outta' there as quiet as we could. Mike drove down the street toward North Main, then he tromped it after we got 'round the last corner before Ashton Highway. He turned off Church and back to Main so he could make sure Clarence's car was still in front of the shop. We thought Mike had what he was lookin' for, so we couldn't figure out why he was so mad.

I asked him where in the hell we were going.

First he cussed us, and then yelled that he wanted **all the photos and the negatives**. After we made damn sure his car was still at the shop, we made a beeline straight to Clarence's house. Mike said there had to be a darkroom someplace, and all the times he'd been to the record shop, he knew it wasn't there. He remembered seeing a storage closet off the carport at Clarence's house... always with a big lock on it. He figured that had to be it!

He knew Mike had been to Clarence's house a lot of times. He'd been to parties as Vince's special guest and figured he knew his way 'round well as anyone. Clarence and Mike weren't friends; fact was, they were far from it. Rumor was that Clarence had even tried to kill Mike. He was real jealous of him where Vince was concerned. Mike said he thought Clarence was *just* not important enough to worry about... in fact, he ignored him and treated him like he was nothin' and wasn't even there. This made Clarence madder than hell... he hated Mike with a passion.

Mike turned on Broadway and drove real slow by the street where Clarence lived. We could see the house, and see if any cars were in the yard... it was all clear. Mike made a coupla' more turns and we were behind Clarence's house... a narrow dirt road with a lot of big trees and underbrush on both sides. There wasn't no cars and nobody was out walkin' - 'especially hot as it was. Mike pulled the rental car off the shoulder and into the bushes real slow. The car was hid... completely outta' sight. Then he reached under the seat and pulled out a coupla' tools.

We got out and waded through the tall bushes 'til we got to Clarence's back yard. Everything was still quiet. I walked 'round the corner of the house to look in the kitchen window and didn't see nobody. Mike went to the carport and started to cut the lock off the storage room door. When he opened that door, he knew he'd hit the jackpot... there was pictures everywhere! A clothesline had 'em hangin' from it just like somebody had just done a load of wash. Mike started openin' boxes... he found more pictures and negatives than he would've ever thought would be in a photo shop. When he reached for another box... it was full of pictures, too... just like all the rest of the boxes. Mike told us he didn't think there'd be so many.... he remembered a few of the pictures, but none, besides the ones of him, were of average people. We couldn't believe there were so many pictures of the rich kids in town. Whoever took 'em sure got those people in some pretty embarrassin' positions... they were all clear and in real good condition... you could tell real easy who they were.

Mike thought sure we'd found the "mother lode" of Vince's blackmail pictures. He started takin' down all the hangin' pictures and put 'em in boxes with the others. Then he picked up all the negatives he could find and put 'em in the boxes with the other negatives. He stacked up the boxes and loaded us up with as many as we could carry. He picked up the rest and we hauled it all back to the car.

Mike said he couldn't believe how lucky we'd been! No fussin'... didn't have to whip nobody... just slip in - slip out... just like takin' candy from a baby. Mike said Vince wouldn't be happy when he found out he'd lost his edge, and Clarence would be *mad as hell* when he found out his blackmail pictures were gone. He doubted Vince or Clarence neither one would report 'em missin'. Mike hadn't just solved his own problem, but now he stood to make a few bucks if his future "in-laws" turned out to be more of a problem than he thought. He told us that it never hurt to have a little security... just like havin' money in the bank.

Mike drove us back to my house. For half an hour we just stood in the yard jokin' around and laughin' about our unbelievable luck!

Mike said it was gettin' late and he had a few things to do before catchin' his plane back to Charlottes-ville. He said he was supposed to be at the lake at a family cookout... he had to get back.

Then he left... where he went or what he did, I don't know. I don't think he'd 've gone back to kill 'em – he got the pictures... that's what he wanted. I don't see he'd have any reason! I just don't know."

"The foregoing statement is correct to the best of my memory, knowledge and belief.

Signed: Donald Burtson"

When Reddick finished reading the document he looked up at the Chief in disbelief. "This is too incredible! Guess he did get all the pictures and negatives?"

"If we can believe any of this statement, it looks like he may have 'em all," the Chief responded.

"If any demand is made, now at least we would know where it came from," Reddick added. "Better still, do you see any way we could get 'em from him?" Reddick asked.

"You mean, assuming this *is* true?" the Chief questioned. He paused for a bit, taking a few long drags off his cigarette. "We may have some leverage," he replied. "What if Mike *did* go on to kill 'em? What if he left his friends and ran across Vince, Clarence and that woman, and just killed them?"

"Why would he?" Reddick questioned. "It's like this report said, he got what he wanted. I can't imagine why he'd need to do that. Besides, from what I've heard about him around town, he's a playboy, a little wild and certainly stuck on himself. I can't imagine him being violent enough to do something like this... not even on his worst day."

"I didn't mean exactly that," the Chief replied. "I just wonder what Mike would be willing to give up if he thought we believed he was somehow involved? Sometimes returning stolen goods could go a long way on a charge of breaking and entering, not to mention a possible charge of murder. It's just a technicality that we most likely could never prove and there's no one around to press charges on the theft if we could. It's the mere accusation that might persuade him to rethink this. Besides, the return of the stuff could be considered an act of cooperation in the biggest murder investigation in the history of our town."

"Yeah, I see what you're getting at," Reddick replied.

As Reddick was passing the report back over the desk to the Chief, the telephone rang. The Chief lifted the receiver to hear his secretary announce a call from the Sheriff's Department.

"Hello, Ben," the Chief answered.

"Investigators in Bascomb County have just called to say they have an ex-con in custody who may be involved in the murders," Ben announced. "I'm on my way over to talk to him... just wanted to know if you might want to come along?"

"Did they say who he was?" the Chief asked.

"A local guy from here," Ben replied. "That's why they called. They wanted to know if we had anything on him. When they told me it was Frederick Johnson, I told 'em he had a rap sheet a mile long... yeah, we know him alright."

"Frederick Johnson?" the Chief repeated. That name *does* ring a bell.

The name pitched through Reddick's body with the force of a hard blow to the gut. The color drained from his face and a sensation of faintness came over him. Luckily the Chief was making a few notes on his desk pad and paid little attention to his telling reaction. Reddick fought to regain his composure, as he knew the Chief was not very likely to overlook the slightest show of emotion.

Reddick heard the Chief tell Ben he would ride over to talk to this Frederick Johnson with him. He'd meet him out front in 15 minutes.

As the Chief was ending the call, he looked up at Reddick with a questioning expression. "Hold on a minute, Ben," he said as he pulled the receiver away from his ear and began to talk to Reddick.

"Didn't you represent a Frederick Johnson five or six years ago?" he questioned.

"Yeah, I did," Reddick answered. "As I recall, he was charged with forgery and had a few other minor charges. 'Best I remember, he was sentenced to seven to ten."

The Chief turned his attention back to the call. "I'm back, Ben. I'll meet you out front in a few minutes," he said.

The Chief replaced the receiver and looked over at Reddick. "I was going to ask you to come along, but since you've represented this guy before, it might create a conflict if he were to ask you to represent him in this."

"What's he been charged with?" Reddick asked, trying not to appear to be overly interested.

"Ben said they were holding him for assault, but with more investigation they hoped to be able to charge him with murder."

"But how would they connect a recent assault with the murders?" Reddick asked.

"It seems that during the assault, Johnson and his accomplice bragged to the victim... telling him how they killed those queers," the Chief continued.

Reddick almost choked. He looked at the Chief and knew he'd better say something before he blushed again, giving the appearance of possible guilt. "Before this is over, there'll be a dozen hoodlums bragging about doing this one. At least half a dozen of the fools will probably even confess," Reddick confidently replied. He was diligently trying to downplay his concern about this critical turn of events. He was not sure how much longer he could maintain his composure. All he could think about now was getting the hell out of the Chief's office.

"Guess I'd better get back to the office and let you get to Ashton," Reddick said as he got up and started toward the door.

"I'll give you a call when we get back," the Chief called after him.

Part 3 ....

Reddick's mind was now in overdrive. He knew Mike Franks more than likely had the coveted pictures and negatives. But that good news was overshadowed by the distinct possibility Freddie could, at any moment, end Reddick's life as he now knew it!

Reddick went back to his office. He had mentally barricaded himself in with tall stacks of folders piled on top of his desk between him and the door. He knew first hand the definition of the term "sweating bullets." Visions of the worst-case scenario kept playing out in his mind. He could see Freddie now, spilling his guts to the Chief. In his mind, he had clear visions of a lynch mob coming to his office to take him away. Perspiration dripped from his face onto a page in Frederick Johnson's folder. What a mess, he thought to himself, what in the hell have I done?

It wasn't much past lunch when Bruce peeked in to see what the Chief had wanted. As he seated himself across the desk, he noticed the perspiration and Reddick's pale complexion. "What's going on... are you okay?"

"Yeah, I just got overheated at lunch, I guess," Reddick replied.

"You sure that's all?' Bruce asked, knowing full well there was definitely more.

"No, really, I'm okay," he replied.

"What did the Chief want?" Bruce asked as he noticed Reddick had the folder in front of him upside down.

"Good news," Reddick replied, trying to put the horror of the bad in the back of his mind. "They have a report maybe Mike Franks is implicated in this and has the pictures. They think a couple of his friends helped him take them out of Clarence Gillespie's house the afternoon of the murder."

"Hey, that *is* good news. Now we just have to figure out how to get them from him, right?"

"Well, it may not be as simple as all that. They also suspect Franks in the murders," Reddick went on. "The Chief said he had a pretty tight alibi, but the stolen goods could be offered up in some sort of deal on the charges of breaking and entering and the theft. Guess we'll just have to see how all this plays out."

"The Chief shares our goals, doesn't he?" Bruce asked almost in a statement rather than a question.

"Oh, yeah, he knows the situation and will certainly do everything in his power to steer this thing our way," Reddick confidently replied. He did feel his statement was solid. He was confident the Chief would do every-thing he could for the Munroe brothers, except break the law.

Bruce got up and threw his jacket across his shoulder. "I'm going over to have a talk with Sandra this afternoon. I don't want to be premature in this, but I think she may let me come back home. Maybe not today, but in the near future," he said, smiling at the possibility.

"Well, good for you... try not to screw it up this time," Reddick said as he smiled back at his brother.

Bruce was out the door. Reddick knew he wouldn't see him again until dinner. He had been debating whether to tell Bruce about Freddie, but could see no real value in divulging more than was absolutely necessary. He'd got-ten himself into this mess, and with everything in him, he would figure how to get out!

Reddick was wasting time. He had accomplished noth-ing since returning from the meeting with the Chief before lunch. It was now mid-afternoon... he figured he would just hang around a while longer, at least until he heard from the Chief.

At a quarter of five Elsie buzzed back to say the Chief was on line one. Reddick quickly picked up the receiver. "Chief, good of you to call."

"Just as we thought, Reddick, this guy is a real hard-ass... he denies everything. He claims to know nothing about the murders... says he was with a friend drinking and doing drugs that day. He can't seem to remember where he got the money to buy the stuff, but he sure remembers using it. Just like all the other cons, he knows his legal rights... seems to know as much about the law as we do. The boys over there said he told them the same story, and it looks like he's sticking to it. Unless we come up with some kind of evidence, there isn't much we can do with him."

"Think he's telling the truth about the murders?" Reddick questioned.

"We may never know. He's as hard as I've ever come across. I don't think the boys over there will be able to get anything from him... they can't seem to intimidate him, he just laughs at 'em," the Chief added. "He's just not buying."

"What do you think they're planning to charge him with?" Reddick asked.

"The only thing they've got is simple assault. He'll prob'ly walk," the Chief replied.

Reddick breathed a little easier. In his heart he hoped never to cross paths with Frederick Johnson again. He hoped that Freddie felt the same way about him. It was logical, thinking about it... if Freddie were to talk about getting money to confront the victims, it would implicate him in the murders. So it only made sense for him to keep his mouth shut. Reddick certainly hoped he would do just that!

Part 4 ....

It was the middle of the following week before the Chief called Reddick about his trip to Charlottesville to talk to Mike Franks. The Chief arranged to meet Reddick at the Hot Spot for lunch.

"Not much to tell," the Chief started after their order was taken. "Ben and I went down to talk to him yesterday. Of course he still denies everything. He denied knowing anything, least of all about any photographs... says to ask his family about his whereabouts that day... claims he was with them at the lake having a family picnic."

"Does it check out?" Reddick asked.

"As far as we can tell, it does. Just between you and me, I don't believe it for a minute. He was here and took those pictures just like Hank said. Earlier this week, I re-interviewed Hank and managed to talk to Robbie. They both deny everything, just like Mike. They're all sticking to the same story... they know all we're doing is speculating and can't prove a thing."

"Did the lab boys get anything when they dusted for prints at Gillespie's house?" Reddick asked.

Yeah, they got a couple of smudges... not enough to ID anybody," the Chief replied.

"Looks pretty much like a dead end, uh?" Reddick stated.

"Well, we might have a new lead, such as it is," the Chief replied. "We had a call a few days ago from one of the employees at the record shop. The guy says he remembered something that might be useful. A few months back, he happened to overhear a conversation between Clarence and an old neighbor of Stevens'. Seems there was a big argument... he said the guy was really angry and accused Clarence of taking some money."

"Anything to it?" Reddick asked.

"We don't know yet. This guy is a doctor and lives up north, in Indiana I think. I've been in contact with a detective up there and he's going to find the man and see what he has to say. May be nothing to it, but I'll let you know when I hear back from him," the Chief said.

"Anything else on Freddie Johnson?" Reddick asked, almost holding his breath. He hated to ask, but damn it, he had to know.

"Nothing. I think Ben told me yesterday they had to let him go. He's probably out on bond 'til his court date on the assault charge. I personally think that's a dead end. This guy just wanted a little attention and was running his mouth, that's all," he said as he wiped his mouth and placed his napkin in his plate.

"Probably so," Reddick replied as he too placed his napkin on the table. "I really appreciate your keeping me up to speed on this, Chief."

"No problem." The Chief hesitated. " By the way, how's your dad been doing, Reddick?"

"About the same, I guess. I talked with Mom this morning and she said he spoke a few words yesterday. It comes and goes."

"And Bruce?" the Chief asked almost under his breath.

"He's cut back on his drinking. You know he's been back home with the wife for a couple of weeks now, since she had the baby," Reddick continued. "Luckily she's been a little too preoccupied to give this mess a lot of thought. This whole thing has hit Bruce pretty hard... he's still in denial about the murders and sick that we haven't recovered the pictures. I wish I could say that the storm is over, but somehow I just don't think it is. I'd feel a lot better if something would give. My guess is this will *never* be over until we get those pictures in our hands," he firmly stated.

"I hate to say it, Reddick, but I think you're right," the Chief replied as they got up from the table and started for the door.

Part 5 ....

Reddick had spent all morning dictating a Complaint and felt he deserved a break. It had been a couple of days since he'd heard from the Chief, so he picked up the phone to dial his number when Elsie buzzed back.

"Yes?" he answered.

"The Chief is on line one," Elsie replied.

"Thanks, I'll take it," Reddick stated as he punched the button for that line. "Hey Chief," he opened. "Just about to call and see if you might want to grab a sand-wich."

"Better not today," the Chief came back. "I just got a call about a homicide across the county line in Bascomb. They don't know if there's a connection yet, but wanted to know if we might have something on the victim. The detective said that it's similar to our investigation, pretty gruesome.

"What do they know?" Reddick asked.

"They just found the guy this morning. He was in his apartment with the heat turned up as high as it would go. They think he might have been dead for a day or two, but in this heat, they won't know 'til they get the results from the autopsy. He was so decomposed they weren't even able to tell how he died," the Chief added.

"What makes them think this has anything to do with the triple murder investigation?" Reddick questioned.

"He's one of the queers," the Chief replied. "Their deputies had questioned him about the murders a few weeks back. I don't think he told them anything they didn't already know. He knew our victims from the clubs and parties in Ashton though. Evidently somebody must have thought he knew something. Or, hell, it may have been over drugs or something totally unrelated... at this point, who the hell knows?"

"Who was he?" Reddick asked.

"I'd never heard of him... name's Don something. I didn't recognize the name and Ben had never heard of him either. Ben told me he was a fairly young guy, worked at a bar just across the county line. He hadn't shown up to work for a day or two and somebody got curious enough to look for him. Maybe we'll know more a little further into the investigation. Ben said he would keep me up to speed, so I'll let you know when I hear something."

"Oh, by the way, any word on the guy from up North?" Reddick asked.

"I talked to the detective up there a day or two ago. He said he did find the guy, but when he questioned him, he denied being down here. He claimed not to be able to remember a thing about the weekend in question... said he didn't know where he was. The detective said the guy *did* admit to knowing both Stevens and Gillespie and it was apparent he had absolutely no use for Gillespie. I guess that puts his name way up the list, since he had a motive and no apparent alibi."

"What do you think?" Reddick asked, as he got a little excited over the possibility.

"Well, our list of suspects seems to be getting longer. Unfortunately, Reddick, as you know, we have the burden of proof, and at this point, we have absolutely no evidence. Until we find something more than what we have, I don't see how we can charge anybody. All we can do is hope somebody screws up and gives themselves away or talks to somebody who will. You know, that does happen occasionally," the Chief said.

"I know how anxious you must be to get a break in this," Reddick told the Chief. "Maybe it won't be much longer. You'll let me know if you hear any more?"

"Oh yeah, I'll let you know when I get any news," the Chief said as he ended the call.

Part 6 ....

　　Days had turned into weeks and weeks into months
and still there was little news to even be hopeful about.
Though Reddick talked with the Chief every day or so,
there were no further developments in the investigation.
After several dozen informants and possible suspects had
been interviewed and interrogated and re-interviewed
and re-interrogated, the progress in the investigation had
come to a halt. It appeared every investigative agency
was leaning toward a different suspect. Few agencies
were in agreement as to how or why the murders occurred as they apparently did. As the political rifts, confusion and difference of opinion continued, the SBI command post was closed and the commissioners appointed
a Special Prosecutor. His job was to organize the reports
and evidence in an effort to find enough proof to charge
somebody with this horrendous crime. After days and
weeks of reviewing the overwhelming number of investigative reports, he too, concluded there were in fact half

a dozen suspects; however, there was still insufficient evidence to charge anyone.

The good news, if any actually existed, was Reddick had not heard a word from Freddie.

The investigation was at an impasse. Reddick had gradually relaxed back into his old routine of a few hours work, socializing with his friends and then calling it a day. Elsie was not very happy with him, but knew in her heart this must be his true nature. Bruce had been back home for almost two months now. He had started drinking heavily again and, of course, Sandra was not happy about that. He'd always had a knack for keeping things on a medium simmer... his lifelong attraction for instability was disturbing.

Reddick seemed to just be waiting for that dreaded day he would either hear from Freddie or would get word the photographs had resurfaced. He was hard pressed to figure which would be the worse nightmare.

Just as Reddick closed a client folder and started to go to lunch, the telephone rang.

"Line one, Reddick. It's the Chief," Elsie announced.

Reddick punched in on line one. "Chief, it's good to hear from you."

"How are things going, Reddick?" the Chief asked.

"It's been a little slow the last couple of weeks. Guess that's a blessing after all the excitement we've had," Reddick answered. "What's new with you?"

"Well, I've just received a folder from Ben over at the Sheriff's Office. When the SBI Command Center closed, they sent all their dormant and uninvestigated leads over to him. It appears they have been trying to revive some of the more interesting ones. I thought you might want to take a look."

"You know I would. Have you had lunch?" Reddick asked as he grabbed his jacket.

"No," replied the Chief. "Why don't you pick up a couple of sandwiches and we can eat while we go over these reports?"

"Be there in a few minutes," Reddick replied as he replaced the receiver and then made his way down the hall.

When he opened the door to step outside, he was faced with a wall of heat. Just as the entire summer had been, it was still unusually hot for mid-October. It took only a minute for Reddick to realize it was far too uncomfortable to walk anywhere. He made his way around the building and into the rear parking lot. This was an excellent excuse to take the car he thought, as he unlocked the door and threw his jacket across the front seat. As he slid in, he started rolling down the windows and started the engine. He paused for a moment to hear the sweet purr of his cherished machine.

Reddick drove a few blocks over to Daisy Queen and picked up a couple sandwiches and proceeded to his meeting with the Chief. Once inside the building, he stopped at the vending machine to get a couple of cokes before he made his way down the hall to the Chief's Office.

Opening the door, Reddick noticed a corner of the desk had been cleared off in preparation for his arrival with lunch. Folders, books and notes pretty much covered the remaining surface of the desk.

"Come in, come in," the Chief said as Reddick stepped inside the small office.

Reddick sat the bagged lunch on the corner of the desk where the Chief had indicated and then handed him a coke. After he sat down, he began to dig in the bag for the sandwiches and napkins.

"This may or may not be anything to get excited about," the Chief said as he opened the folder containing the most recent information from the Sheriff's Department. "I read over some of the introduction, but haven't gotten down to any startling new developments yet. From what I can tell, the more promising leads have pretty much dried up for every department investigating these murders. When the SBI closed up shop, they transferred a file box full of untouched leads to the Sheriff's Department. As the detectives were sorting through and reviewing all the old tips, and more or less grasping at straws, they came upon several dormant reports that stood out. At the time they were taken by the SBI, some of the reports seemed to be so far out in left field they were discounted without any investigation. But now, since most of the more credible leads have long been exhausted, the detectives thought some of them might be worth looking at."

"When the Sheriff's deputies delved into what they had inherited, they recognized the names of several prominent citizens as having made some of the reports. This, in itself, peeked their interest and gave the reports instant credibility."

"This has turned out to be a treasure trove of new information. Though the reports were several months old, the deputies immediately began taking new statements and conducting interviews. These newly discovered leads had pumped a measure of energy back into the investigation," the Chief said as he finally picked up his sandwich for the first time. After taking a few bites and having a drink of his coke, he continued.

"The new focus of the investigation seems to be the Pervis Cottages on the south side of town. The boys are real familiar with that location. The place has a reputation for wild parties, drugs, booze, women, the whole works. I understand the County boys are always having to go down there to investigate complaints... not what you'd call a family atmosphere."

After another bite of his lunch, the Chief continued with the more interesting parts of his news. "Some of the reports suggested the murders may have been committed at that location, maybe in the main house... but after a little more digging, the boys now think the more likely murder site could be one of the cottages at the complex."

"You've got to be kidding! If there's anything to this, it's going to open a Pandora's box as far as suspects and motives. Holy shit, Chief, how likely do you think this might be?"

"It seems to be a new game, Reddick, we don't know what the hell to believe yet. We're just going to have to let this thing play out and see where it leads," the Chief replied. "Ben told me the investigators weren't too surprised when they couldn't get any information from the owners of the cottages. For that matter, the employees were less than eager to answer any questions. Ben said that everybody down there seemed to be uncooperative and they have historically been on the wrong side of the law. Even if they were to give the deputies any information, it would most likely be false or misleading. Bottom line is, you can't trust anything they say."

"Ben told me this revived investigation had started off real slow and once the preliminary interviews had been done, the neighbors and other people who might have some connection to the cottages were still less than anxious to tell them what they knew. The detectives got some information and a few clues. It's hard to know just how valid the statements and information might be until we have time to check it all out... it takes a long time to sift through the leads and try to distinguish what might be relative and what's worthless," the Chief said as he finished off his sandwich.

"Is there any known connection between these cottages and the victims?" Reddick asked.

"One of the employees admitted she recognized a photograph of Stevens and Gillespie. They'd been there for a party not too long before the murders. She claimed she'd never seen the woman before," the Chief replied as he turned the first page in the folder.

Reddick's mind was spinning. So far there was absolutely no evidence that Freddie and his slimy friend were anywhere around the crime scene... matter of fact, they had no evidence against anybody. But with the possibility of a new crime scene location and the evidence and information that would be developed with that, together with new searches being conducted, Reddick wondered what the chances would be of finding something to implicate Freddie. If that were to happen, it would no doubt lead back to his doorstep concerning the Friday night before the murders. After quickly weighing the number of suspects and the probability of any connection, Reddick concluded that what little information he personally possessed, together with what little he had gleaned from Bruce, in all probability would be inconsequential.

"If there is an ounce of truth to this, it could put an entirely different spin on the case," Reddick stated. "I didn't say anything that night at the crime scene, Chief, but I did notice something that would indicate the murders didn't happen down there."

"What are you talking about, Reddick?"

"Well, remember how the woman's blouse was pulled back over her shoulders and wadded up in the back with both arms still in the sleeves?"

"Yeah, what about it?" the Chief looked over at him somewhat puzzled.

"Think about it, Chief. The brassiere was at the side of the body, near the feet. How could it have been taken off without first removing her arms from the blouse?"

"Damn, guess you have a point. If the victims were killed there, there would be no reason to re-dress her. If that's the case, somebody went to a lot of trouble to alter the area around the bodies; may be trying to mislead us into believing the motive could be something other than what it was."

"What's the possibility the entire area where the bodies were found was a set up?" Reddick asked. "What would motivate somebody to commit such a brutal murder then go to all that trouble unless they had more to hide?"

The Chief ignored the question and focused on the second page in the folder. "This first interview is from a neighbor close to the Pervis Cottages. They told the investigator that a lot of renovation work was going on at one of the cabins a few days before they read about the killings. They thought that was unusual because the owners had never made any improvements to speak of since buying the place. Common sense would dictate a major renovation would've been scheduled for the off-season

months. No logical business person would make them during the busiest time of the year!"

"I guess that makes sense," Reddick replied.

The Chief quickly turned to the next page. "The next
interview was from a couple of the cleaning people. They
were actually scared out of their wits to talk to the detectives, so the Sheriff sent old Joe down to talk to 'em.
Black folks don't seem to trust us much anyway. Says
here, as Joe reported, they were instructed to clean one
of the cabins first thing on Wednesday morning, the 20th of
July. When they went in, the cabin was all torn up. Blood
was everywhere and the bedclothes and shower curtain
were gone. One of the chairs was broken and the ceiling had been blasted with a shotgun. The women said it
scared them so bad they went running out the door and
flatly refused to go back in. They said no amount of money would be enough to get them back in that cabin. The
Chief looked over at Reddick. "I doubt they'd be lying
about something like that."

"It would be one hell of a coincidence if these cottages
and the murders aren't related, " Reddick replied

"I tend to agree with the boys from the SBI... this is
almost too far out in left field to believe. With this possible turn of events, I can understand why the detectives
are being so skeptical though. The Sheriff is getting so
much heat to solve it, they're willing to look at anything...
they're like the rest of us, they just want to put this mess
to bed."

"Understandable," Reddick chimed in.

As he turned to the next page in the folder, the Chief continued. "When the deputies started checking the guest register, if you want to call it that, the entries for the weekend of the murders were sketchy at best. The night clerk says cabin six was rented to a stranger in the wee hours of Sunday morning, July 17. Since the guy paid cash, the clerk didn't require identification. When the detectives asked him about it, the clerk said that was what he was told to do. He just followed instructions."

"They got nothing?" Reddick questioned. "I can't believe they got no ID at all."

"Goes on to say cabin six was occupied by two people. When the car left for a while Sunday, someone noticed the tag was from out-of-state. Does not say which one though - guess that gives us 49 to choose from," the Chief smiled. "Does not give a check-out time, or date for that matter. Says here the cabin was next rented the 4th day of August. That's close enough to two and a half weeks, don't you think?"

"Sounds like it pretty much matches what the neighbor was saying. Two and a half weeks would give ample time to cover up a mess," Reddick added. Supposing this could be a possibility, if you figure in what the cleaning ladies said, the bodies could have been in the cabin until Monday, or even Tuesday."

"It's starting to add up in my mind," the Chief said as he turned back to the report from the maids.

"Supposing the victims *were* killed at the cottages, why would the killer then move the bodies? Why not just leave them there? With the kind of management you've described, probably nobody would ever know who did it," Reddick said.

"Who said the *killer* moved the bodies?" the Chief quipped as he studied the report.

"I fail to see why anyone else would go to that much trouble," Reddick hesitantly replied.

"Well, the one reason I can think of is those cottages, according to Ben, are right on the brink of being closed down. An incident of this magnitude would definitely be the last straw. I don't think the Pervises could stand that kind of heat, even if they were totally innocent in this," the Chief stated. "From the descriptions given here, the old man who owns the place is an alcoholic. He married a much younger woman who likes to party. She no doubt has an alcohol problem and from this report, could possibly be a drug user to boot. I'd imagine they wouldn't be able to continue their lifestyle, as it is, if they were closed down."

"Very good point," Reddick acknowledged. "So, you're suggesting that whoever was in the car with the victims on Sunday afternoon took them to the cottages, perhaps for a party or some other unknown reason, and then killed them."

"I think it's a possibility," the Chief replied.

"Then you think that crowd at the cottages found the bodies, moved them, cleaned up the mess and went on just like nothing had happened?"

"Why not?" the Chief answered. "It probably was nothing to them... I imagine their objective would be to protect themselves. They probably would have been smart enough to arrange things where the bodies were found to put the investigators off track... Ben said they were misleading scoundrels. You would have to admit, the Voodoo effect that somebody tried to plant certainly had the boys going."

"Well, it all sounds possible, Chief, but that opens a brand new can of worms, doesn't it?"

"Yes, I guess it does. The obvious questions still remain, in addition to a fresh batch of suspects," he stated as he sat back in his chair and lit a cigarette. "One thing is for sure, we can't expect to get any help from the crowd at the cottages. As I see it, the only chance we have of solving this thing is to ID the man in the back seat of Stevens' car. Once we do that, we'd probably have the motive. Right now we have too many to choose from, but with that ID, it could narrow it down to possibly one. It might be easier to ID him if we could figure out why the woman was with them and how she fits into this puzzle... she could be the key to the whole thing."

Reddick swallowed hard. He still didn't feel comfortable telling the Chief what Bruce had told him in regard to the woman. There was no real reason for his silence on this matter, except that maybe he still knew something that had yet to be revealed.

"Was there any common thread in the description of the man in the back seat of Stevens' car, from the three witnesses who claimed to have seen them Sunday afternoon?" Reddick asked.

"One of 'em, during the second interview, made a positive ID of Mike Franks. He claims he's absolutely sure it was Franks. To be honest, the investigators found it a little strange, since he failed to ID him during the first interview. They suspect some kind of conflict between him and Franks," the Chief stated.

"If that's true, he probably knows a lot more than he's telling."

"I personally think with what we know about the whereabouts of Mr. Franks, not to mention his seemingly airtight alibi, we'd be wasting our time even going there," the Chief continued.

"The other male witness appears to be very credible and claims to know Franks... but says he didn't recognize the man in the back seat. He was positive it was *not* Franks," the Chief said.

"The most troubling statement," he paused as he took a long drag off the cigarette, "was made by the most credible witness. The lady who saw the Stevens' car going north on highway 191 said she was sure two men were in the back seat. What she said that was not released to the press was that she saw the other car – the one supposedly belonging to the woman - parked where it was found. She also saw a black sedan parked at the side of the road with a man inside. She said he was eyeing the traffic and appeared to be waiting for someone. Now, if that is fact, it would leave one man with Stevens and another in the black sedan to account for after they picked up the woman, if indeed that was what happened." The Chief took another long drag off his cigarette and put it out in the ashtray. "Lots and lots of questions," he said as he got up from his chair.

"The more information you get, the more complicated this thing becomes," Reddick stated as he, too, stood from his chair and stepped toward the door. "You'll keep me posted on any developments?"

"Yeah, we should be getting more later this afternoon or first thing in the morning. Ben told me the detectives would be out taking statements this afternoon," the Chief replied.

Reddick was out the door and back into the heat of the day. He didn't even bother going back to the office. This overload of new information had just made his head spin... and all he wanted to do was to find a peaceful place to digest it and have a nice quiet drink. He happened to know a place on the west side of town that would do nicely.

Part 7 ....

Now that the investigation was focusing on the Pervis Cottages south of town, it was as though someone had poured water on an already smoldering fire. Some of the people in that area who had called in tips months earlier were miffed at having been ignored for so long... they blamed the failure to resolve the case in a timely manner on that fact. Others in the area, especially those directly connected to the cottages, still wanted to have nothing to do with the new interest in the case.

For weeks the detectives tried to dig up anyone who might have seen anything unusual the weekend of the murders. Too much time had passed... people simply couldn't remember details from that long ago. As far as questioning the guests who were at the cottages at the time, the absence of records made that impossible as well. As expected, neither the employees nor the "regular" party people who might have possibly been there that weekend, were willing to contribute anything to the investigation at all. The degree of intentional amnesia was just phenomenal.

Finally, the Sheriff's Department did receive an anonymous tip on who may have been responsible for moving the bodies. The follow-up on that piece of information proved to be most difficult.

It was reported that three men were involved in transferring the bodies to the location where they were discovered. The oldest of the three was Judson Bennett, who apparently was a "regular fixture" at the cottages. The detectives had questioned him earlier in the investigation when they were informed the cottages might have been the actual crime scene. At that time, they suspected him to be more than a casual friend of young Mrs. Pervis, wife of the cottages' owner. The detectives learned that he, under her direction, provided the pickup truck used to transport the bodies.

They also learned he was assisted by a relative of one of the owners and one of his friends. By the time the detectives got around to questioning the three, the latter two had already fallen off the face of the earth. The relative was nowhere to be found and his friend had moved to the other side of the continent... supposedly fearing for his life.

Rumor was, upon receipt of this new information, the Sheriff had immediately dispatched his chief detective to California to interview the relative's friend. The detective had done much better than just an interview; he brought the witness back to town to be interrogated.

The entire affair, of course, was conducted under extremely tight security. The scheduling for his return and subsequent questioning was on a need-to-know basis within the department. No one outside the department was aware of the event until it was completed and the witness had been returned safely to California.

****

It had been a couple of weeks after the secret interview had taken place. The skies looked like snow, but it was only rain that had been making everyone miserable all day. The City of Four Seasons had proven to be only two this particular year – summer and winter.

Having been given a heads-up call from Ben a few days before, the Chief had been impatiently awaiting the receipt of the brief. It was pushing 5:00 p.m. on the last Friday in the month of November, and the Chief had given up hope of receiving the report this late in the week. He felt like he'd been waiting an eternity on a report that, at best, was only going to result in revealing who had moved the bodies. It would, by no stretch of the imagination, reveal who had committed the murders. None-the-less, he was eager to get any new information on the case.

Just as the Chief was pulling on his jacket and getting ready to leave, his secretary opened the door and greeted him with the long awaited report.

He was surprised and a bit anxious that the folder had come so late in the day. He immediately picked up the phone to call Reddick as he enthusiastically opened the envelope.

The Chief had removed the report and was scanning the first page when he realized the Law Offices of Munroe, Munroe & Munroe had closed for the day. He quickly dialed Reddick's home number. He got no answer there either. As a last resort, the Chief dialed the number out at the Lodge. One of the guys was able to pull Reddick away from the table that happened to be between games.

"Hello," the Chief heard Reddick say.

"Reddick, I just got the report. Care to meet me at the Club and take a look at it?" the Chief asked, already knowing the answer.

"I'm on my way," Reddick replied as he finished his drink and grabbed his coat. He had parked as close to the front door as he could, but he was chilled to the bone by the time he got to his car. It was generally an easy drive to the Club, but he had not accounted for the rush hour traffic and the miserable weather.

After Reddick made the steep grade at Browning Avenue, and rounded the curve, he saw the Chief had pulled into the drive before him. He had already reached the door with the report folder and was juggling the door key and a cup. By the time Reddick made it to the door, the Chief had it open and managed to get inside out of the rain.

"And we complained about sunshine and a little heat!" Reddick quipped.

"Yeah, can you believe it?" the Chief chuckled.

The men hung up their wet coats and turned on the kitchen light. They were soon sitting at the table with the long awaited report before them.

"Hot off the press?" Reddick asked as he watched the Chief remove the report from its covering.

"Apparently so," the Chief replied. "I called you as soon as it arrived. I hope, after all the hoop-la, it's worth the wait."

Reddick waited as he watched the Chief scan down the first page. This page was generally an update of the situation and the status of the case thus far. As the Chief finished reading it, he handed it to Reddick... and started to read the second.

"Ever heard the name Danny Mason?" the Chief asked.

"No, don't think I have. Why, is that the mystery guy?" Reddick asked.

"Judging from this, he's one scared puppy. They traded him immunity from prosecution in exchange for his testimony."

"Good trade for us," Reddick said. "Punishment couldn't be much for moving a dead body."

"He says here, the law is the least of his worries."

"This guy participated in the destruction of evidence in the largest murder investigation in our town's history, *and the law was the least of his worries?*" Reddick mocked.

With that, Reddick rose from his chair and walked around the table so he could read over the Chief's shoulder. He soon pulled a chair around and the Chief angled the paper so Reddick could read alongside him. The third page of the report contained the real meat of the interview - a time line of events.

"Listen to his statement," the Chief broke in. "He states that his friend Benny called him sometime after work on Monday, July 18. Benny said that a relative had called him a little earlier that day. She told him there had been an accident at the cottages and asked if he would come and help haul off a few things. He asked me if I would come along and help, so I told him that I would. He picked me up about 9:00 p.m. and we rode over to the cottages. Benny's relative and her friend were there to meet us at one of the cottages, number 6, I think. The friend - they called him Judd, already had his pickup truck backed up to the cottage door. We walked around the truck and stepped inside the cottage. Once inside, Judd pulled out a sawed off shotgun and said that he would not hesitate to kill us on the spot if we gave him any trouble. "Just look around, boys," he said, "if you think I'm kidding!" Just as he said that, he turned on the light inside the cabin. Dead bodies were everywhere! Benny and I both panicked. We knew the two men - Gillespie and Stevens from the record shop in town... but we had no idea who the woman was. Benny's relative came in about that time with a tarp and told Judd to relax, she said we were smart boys and knew to keep our mouths shut."

"It looked like a fight had taken place, there was blood everywhere. Stevens' body was on the floor over in front of the small bathroom door. Gillespie was on the floor between the twin beds, and the woman was on the bed, partially naked. We were so scared; we just did what we were told. We carried the bodies and all their personal effects to the bed of the pickup and covered them up with the tarp. It just took a few minutes. Then Judd told us to get in the truck. He drove across to Highway 176 and headed south. I don't know that area very well, but I know we turned onto a couple of dirt roads before we stopped to unload the bodies. It was dark, but with the truck lights and the smell, I could tell it was a trash dump. We unloaded the bed of the truck and got out of there as quick as we could. Judd threatened us all the way back to the cottages. He told us if we ever told anybody about this, he would make sure we would be accused of the murders. If the law didn't take care of us – *he sure as hell would!*"

It was noted the investigators then showed Danny the "crime scene photos." His reaction was solemn silence. When he was shown the picture of the woman, tears rolled down his cheeks.

"We didn't do this! We were scared and in too big a hurry to get them out of the truck. We just pulled them off the tailgate in a pile and took off. He must have gone back!"

'The question was presented to the witness: Do you think Judd committed the murders?'

"I don't know. Just before Benny disappeared, he told me that Judd was full of shit. He would never have the guts to do anything like that. He was just a bully and liked to brag and act tough. Benny told me to just keep my mouth shut and not worry about him. He said a few days later that his relative told him Judd didn't do it."

Danny was asked if he knew where Benny was. 'He seemed to "cloud up" and meekly said he didn't. He said he was afraid Judd might have killed him…. that was the reason he was so scared.'

There wasn't much more to the report. Mason's signature and the 'Attested to By' witness list were on the last page.

The Chief and Reddick fell silent when they had finished reading the report. The Chief sat back in his chair and lit a cigarette as Reddick reviewed the last few pages of the report with a sense of amazement.

"This is just too damned incredible not to be true," Reddick stated.

"It sure fits with everything else the boys have learned about the cottages in the last few weeks," the Chief replied. "Do you remember the report Ben sent containing the interviews from the cleaning ladies?"

"Yeah, didn't they say they were told to clean the cottage on Wednesday morning?"

"The best I can remember, that's what they said. It certainly could fit with the time line. But, do you happen to remember if they said which cottage they were asked to clean?" the Chief asked.

"I don't remember, but if they didn't, I bet the Sheriff's boys will have that answer before the weekend's over. Those cottages will be put under a microscope now that this information has come to light."

"If my memory serves me right, that report also said one of the guests at the cottages that weekend had an out-of-state tag on his car. Was that not for cottage # 6?" the Chief asked.

"Here in this report," Reddick said as he flipped back through the pages, "Mason said it was cottage # 6. I only know of one of the suspects who lives outside the state."

"And he can't seem to remember where he was," the Chief added. "How very convenient for him."

"It could be possible for *any* of the other suspects to have been with somebody having an out-of-state tag," Reddick said, thinking of Freddie and hoping to eliminate him as a suspect. "Chief, have you heard anything recently in regard to Frederick Johnson?"

"Reddick, the last time I talked with any of the detectives from Ashton, they said that Frederick Johnson had dropped out of sight. He got probation on that charge of assault and when he walked, he kept right on going. His probation officer hasn't heard from him since his release. Besides, I never seriously considered him to be a suspect anyway."

"What about Franks?" Reddick asked.

The Chief took the last puff of his cigarette and ground it out in the ashtray. " I know a guy who works Vice in Charlottesville," he stated. "He's been keeping an eye on Franks for us. You know Franks married that little rich girl a few months back... big wedding, I understand. Anyway, he's been managing his new father-in-law's downtown store the last few months. Everything seems to be quiet so far, but word has it the old man is not too crazy about the situation. One wrong move, and he'll show Franks the street."

"Guess he still has the pictures?" Reddick asked as he put the report folder back together.

"I haven't heard a word," the Chief replied. "The detective in Charlottesville is trying to get a lead on some of his friends. If he can find out who he hangs out with, maybe he can get something to go on, but no luck so far."

"He may sit on those pictures forever... or, for all we know, he may have already gotten rid of them."

"I wouldn't count on that if I were you," the Chief said as he checked his watch. "I don't think he's stupid *or* that admirable. If I were guessing, I would think he would keep 'em to fall back on if his new golden goose flies the coop. After all, he could do the same thing our victims were doing. There's just no way to know how much money he could pull down in a blackmail scheme. From the report, he has enough material to make a killing, but there's nothing we can do 'til he makes a move - and we may have a long wait."

Reddick looked out the kitchen window when he got up to move his chair back. It was already black dark. "I didn't realize it was getting so late," he said.

"I've gotta' go, too... the missus is going to be wondering what happened to me. She already says she has a hard time recognizing me and if I'm not careful, she'll file a missing persons report on me," the Chief chuckled as he picked up the folder.

"We should have something on the cottages by the first part of the week. I'll give you a call when I hear from Ben," the Chief added.

Reddick reached for their coats. He handed one to the Chief and put on the other as he turned off the kitchen light and followed the Chief out the door. The rain had slacked a little, but they noticed a few flakes of snow in the headlights as they slowly made their way out the drive.

Part 8 ....

The weather had remained cold and miserable throughout the weekend. Reddick's time was spent preparing for trial in a civil matter to be heard the following week. He was having a difficult time concentrating on the defense with so much new information concerning the murder investigation to mentally sort through.

The information thus far concerning the Pervis Cottages was convincing enough for Reddick to believe the murders had been committed there. He believed Mason and his friend helped move the bodies. The big questions remained, who killed the victims and why?

Monday had been just as dreary as the preceding weekend. Reddick had been working so diligently on his case he hardly noticed the entire day had passed and he had heard nothing from the Chief. He decided he'd punished himself enough on this case, so he collected his coat and briefcase and headed for the door. When he walked by her desk, Elsie was still typing the final draft of his Summary. "I'll look over that tomorrow," he said.

She looked up at him with that familiar knowing smile and told him to have a nice evening.

****

Reddick felt more rested on Tuesday morning. The sun was shining and he had almost completed his summation for his upcoming court trial. When he entered the office, the first thing he smelled was the coffee. He spoke briefly to Elsie, and then continued down the hall with his cup of fresh brew and the <u>Tribune</u> tucked under his arm. As he walked past Bruce's door, he noticed it was partially open and the lights had not been turned on. He had not been in the office since last Thursday. It just made Reddick sick to think he was on another binge. He made a mental note to call him later to make sure he was okay.

Reddick had just sat down and opened the paper when Elsie buzzed. "Yes?" he asked when he punched the intercom button.

"It's the Chief on line one," she answered.

Reddick pushed the button and greeted the Chief, "Good morning."

"Good morning," he replied. "Just got word from Ben about that cottage. It *was* Cottage # 6."

"What did they find out?" Reddick anxiously asked.

"Nothing - it's gone."

"Gone - what are you talking about?"

"When the county boys were down there the middle of October doing their investigation, they noticed one of the cabins had been renovated... but they didn't pay much attention to which one. They went down this weekend to take another look and found a flagstone patio and a couple of picnic tables where a cabin used to be. The cabin numbers relative to the patio indicated that Cottage # 6 was missing," the Chief stated.

"I'll be damned. What can they do?" Reddick asked.

"Nothing that I know of. The place hadn't been declared a crime scene and the boys had fulfilled their search when they got a warrant the middle of October. Since the cottages are private property, looks like we have no say. As far as I can tell, the circumstances have allowed the people down there to screw us once again."

"So bottom line is, nobody can be convicted of this crime because we still have no evidence. We got squat!"

"Well," the Chief hesitated, "we still have one strong suspect remaining - the guy in Indiana. I know it's a long shot, but he did have a motive and no alibi. He'd probably have an out-of-state tag on his vehicle if he drove down. Maybe with a miracle - we could get him to confess. Then if we could come up with enough circumstantial evidence to go along with his confession, we might be able to get a conviction," he said with a chuckle.

"That's a lot of 'ifs and maybes,' Chief," Reddick chuckled back.

"Seriously, it may be wishful thinking, but right now that's all we've got. I think I'll make a trip up there to talk to him myself. If I confront him with this new information and make him think we can prove he was in town that weekend, he might cave. At this point, I don't see how it could possibly hurt.

"I agree, Chief," Reddick affirmed. "You might as well be the one to break this case. I'll be anxious to learn what you find out, so keep me posted."

"I'll probably go up in the next day or two... and don't worry, I'll let you know as soon as I learn anything," the Chief replied.

"Call any time," Reddick said as he finished his conversation with the Chief.

Part 9 ....

The Chief made his travel reservations and arranged for the detective in Cumberland, Indiana, to meet him at the airport. He was scheduled to arrive on flight 601 at 1:10 p.m. on Friday afternoon. The plans were, that he and the detective would go directly to see Dr. Peter Wellington at his office on West 10th Street.

The size of the city, together with the traffic congestion, was almost overwhelming for the Chief. He was used to less populace and at a much slower pace. He said nothing, but felt relieved he was not the one maneuvering in the mid-day traffic. He and the detective decided to grab a quick lunch before their visit with the doctor. It gave them a chance to discuss the investigation and exchange ideas on a game plan.

When they arrived at the office and flashed their credentials, the receptionist quietly escorted them back to the doctor's private office. After a very brief wait, Dr. Wellington came into the room. The detective introduced the Chief to the doctor and explained he had traveled a great distance to ask him a few more questions about the murders.

Though the doctor appeared to be calm and reserved, there seemed to be an underlying anxiety that a detective from home would travel so far just to talk to him. He explained to the officers he had told them all he knew and had assumed when he last spoke with the local detective, the matter of the murders had been put to rest as far as he was concerned.

The Chief opened his briefcase and removed a well-worn notebook. "We have recently received new information on the triple homicide and hoped you might be able to help us clear up a few details," he said as he opened his notebook and took out his pen.

The doctor's demeanor instantly changed. "I don't know what I can tell you... I've already told you all I know," he firmly stated. His initially gracious attitude started to fade.

"We have information that you and a friend arrived in town during the early hours on Sunday, July 17th," the Chief began. "The two of you checked into the Pervis Cottages south of town." The Chief then began flipping pages in his notebook as if he were looking for something. "Says here that you checked into cottage # 6," the Chief continued as he checked for any telling expression on the doctor's face.

"**That's a lie!**" he shouted. "**I told you before, I was not in Carolina then.**" The color had completely drained from the doctor's face. He looked like he had seen a ghost.

"We have it on good authority," the Chief continued, "you and your friend went to see Vince Stevens and Clarence Gillespie about some money Gillespie had stolen from you."

For a few minutes the doctor said nothing. He sat motionless, staring at the top of his desk. It was as though his eyes glazed over with a memory or a scene from the past.

"Dr. Wellington?" the Chief said, trying to bring the good doctor back from his daydream.

"I was not in Carolina. I was here in Cumberland that weekend," the doctor finally stated. "The entire weekend... I didn't go anywhere."

"Sir, we need to know exactly where you were and who might corroborate your statement," the detective broke in.

The doctor looked up, straight at the detective. " I was out raising hell with my buddy, Leo," he said, as if that statement would resolve the entire issue.

"Leo who?" the detective shot back.

"Leo... I'll go get the information... I guess you'll want his address, too," he begrudgingly muttered as he rose to leave the office.

The detective got up, too, thinking the doctor was going to bolt.

"I'm just going to the file cabinet to get Leo's folder, I'll be back in a minute," he said as he motioned to the detective to return to his seat.

As Peter walked down the hall, he knew he must mentally suppress any memories or emotions connected with the weekend in question. He must detach himself completely from everything concerning his friend Vince. Now it was very important he only concentrate on certain things, just as he and Leo had discussed. Knowing this day might eventually come, they were more than prepared. Since that weekend, he and Leo had many long conversations on how to best handle the situation.

The doctor wiped his eyes on his lab jacket before he got to the reception area. He walked directly over to the patient file cabinet and located Leo's information. He tried as best he could to keep his back to the receptionist... he didn't want her to know he was upset or that anything might be wrong.

"Please tell Mr. Crosby I'll be with him in a few minutes," he quietly said to her as he left the area and headed back to his office.

By the time he reached his office door, he had regained his composure. He laid the folder on top of his desk as he took his seat. "Leonardo D'Santos," he said. He then provided the address and other information requested by the investigators.

The local detective informed the doctor this information would be checked out. He advised him not to leave town until it could be confirmed.

After noting the new information, the detectives politely thanked the doctor and made their way out of his office. Once they were outside, the detective and the Chief agreed the doctor was visibly upset, but neither was sure it was due to guilt.

"If we had one witness or an ounce of proof we could have used, I believe he would have been ready to fold," the Chief said as they walked back to the car.

Once back in the parking lot, the local officer called the station with the tag numbers for each vehicle parked there. When Dr. Wellington's car was identified, the detective retrieved a Polaroid from the trunk of his car and took a snapshot.

"If we can locate this Leo character and ID his car, maybe your people at the scene can place one or the other of them as having been there," the detective said as he got back in the car.

They pulled out of the parking lot and the detective drove straight to the address the doctor had given him... he was familiar with that part of town. It was not particularly crime-ridden, but a bit older and could easily slide that way, depending on influence.

As they drove past Leo's house, they saw no vehicle at all. They slowly drove to the end of the street and turned around. When they came back up to the house number, a late model Chevrolet was just pulling into the drive... they whipped in behind it. As they each got out and waved their badges, they began to identify themselves.

"Are you Leonardo D'Santos?" the local detective asked.

"What can I do for you?" was Leo's reply.

"Just wanted to ask you a few questions," the Chief chimed in.

As the local detective started the questioning, the Chief inconspicuously jotted down his tag number and got a brief description of his car. Much to his disappointment, the car appeared to be too new... he doubted seriously that Leo could have owned this car at the time of the murders.

When the detective had finished his round of questioning, the Chief commented on the new car. Leo told them he had recently purchased it. He was very vague when the Chief asked him about the vehicle he owned before this one.

The information Leo gave them was pretty much a carbon copy of what Dr. Wellington had told them earlier in the day. They didn't seem to be getting anywhere with these two.

When the detective and the Chief got downtown, they compared notes on the interviews. It was very clear to them their alibis were well rehearsed. The Doctor and Leo were too vague with exactly where they were at the time of the murders; they were only sure they were to-gether.

The detective ran a background check on the Doctor and neither man was surprised that it turned up nothing. He then ran a rap sheet on Leo... it could have easily been a book. After printing the best mug shot he could find, he ran the plate on Leo's car, only to find out it was a new tag issued with his new car. He did a little more checking and came up with the make and model of the car Leo had traded in. Unfortunately, he was not able to get the color.

The Chief and the detective had gathered as much information as possible and discussed the two interviews until well into the night. It was disappointing they could not nail the doctor with positive proof, but both men felt good about what they had accomplished. They agreed the Doctor and Leo were very likely guilty of committing the murders, but proving their suspicions would be a horse of a different color.

The detective drove the Chief to his motel room. Before leaving, he told the Chief he would pick him up early enough the next morning so they could have breakfast before his 9:30 a.m. flight out.

The Chief got very little sleep. The events of the day kept running through his mind like a movie. He tried to remember the expression on the Doctor's face when he told him he'd been seen in town that weekend, though Leo showed absolutely no emotion when the local detective said the same thing to him. Leo is just cold, the Chief thought. He truly suspected Leo was the one who actually killed the trio, but he had no doubt the Doctor had been there and was an accomplice.   He had a gut feeling the Doctor had a strong emotional bond with Stevens; he just could not figure what the nature of that bond was.

****

A few days after the Chief returned from Indiana, he circulated an FYI report to the various agencies giving them the details and new information from the trip. They had been so good keeping him up-to-speed; he felt he should, by all means, give them the scoop on his little investigation.

He had, of course, already discussed the trip in its entirety with Reddick. He took care of that matter the afternoon of his return. At that time, he confided to Reddick that he and the Cumberland detective agreed that the Doctor and D'Santos were likely the killers.

Unfortunately, when he provided Ben with the vehicle descriptions and the photograph of Dr. Wellington's car, no one at the cottages recognized, or would admit they recognized, either car, much less the photographs of either suspect.

The Chief felt confident he knew who had committed the murders and why, but he doubted seriously he would ever be able to prove it.

Uneasy Reckoning ....

The investigation dragged on. With no new leads and absolutely no evidence, the general consensus was:

*- We strongly suspect **who**,*
*- We think we know **why**, and*
*- We are pretty sure we know **where**,* but
We Simply Can't Prove It!

Months had turned to years. The community had even stopped complaining that the murders had not been solved. Leadership at some of the agencies had changed, and what little crime scene evidence there was had been lost or disposed of. The likelihood there would ever be resolution, much less a conviction in these murders, was nil. The most horrendous triple murder in the history of the county, and no one would even be charged! There would be no justice in this. For whatever reason or whomever may be responsible, this loss of life would never be vindicated.

The Law Offices of Munroe, Munroe and Munroe had, from all appearances, settled back into the comfortably reputable firm it was known to be before the triple murders had occurred. Reddick seemed to be turning out a little more work under the direction and close supervision of Elsie, or so she liked to think. She knew his father would expect nothing less. It was a true shame no one, not even Elsie, could do much with Bruce. The hope was, there would be some improvement in his behavior as he got a little older; however, only time would tell. The senior partner in the firm remained in failing health due to a stroke he had suffered back before the murders. His total recovery wasn't at all expected, though he did have many "good" days.

The Chief now saw and talked with Reddick weekly, in addition to the get-togethers at the Club. As a result of the many consultations and deliberations around the time of the murders, there was a special closeness between the two. Reddick supposed the Chief, being his father's best friend prior to his stroke, missed that relationship. Reddick didn't mind. He enjoyed the Chief's company... he had always respected and admired him.

****

There was still a chill in the air as Reddick left for the office. The winter had been unusually brutal, not normal for the mountains of Western North Carolina. Generally there would have been a snowfall or two, but they usually weren't a big factor... they'd last a day or two and then just melt away. This year, however, there hadn't been any warm sunshine to melt the snow. It had remained on the ground to welcome the next snowfall, and then the next after that. Everyone was sick of snow and sick of the cold temperatures. This year winter had overstayed its welcome... everyone was ready for spring.

As Reddick opened his car door, he noticed the trees lining his drive appeared to be budding. This was surely a sign spring was just around the corner. This one small observation seemed to spark a more optimistic outlook – not exactly spring fever, but at least an improvement over the gloom of the cold, bleak winter.

He was first to arrive at the office. He started a pot of coffee and then went into the reception area to pick up a folder of documents Elsie had typed for him the day before. He sat down at the table in the break area to read over the documents while he waited for the coffee to finish perking. He did not have to be in Court until later in the morning. He poured a cup of coffee, put the folder of documents under his arm, together with the newspaper and headed down the hall to his office.

He sat down and cleared off a space so he could spread the paper. When he unfolded it, his heart almost stopped. There was Freddie's picture - all over the front page.

"Local Man Arrested - Charged with Forgery"

With his heart now racing, Reddick quickly scanned the article. He breathed a sigh of relief when he saw no mention of the triple murders. His blood still ran cold with regret when he thought about that Friday night meeting with Freddie and the uncertainty of his involvement in the murders. It was amazing how an unrelated incident could bring about such emotional discomfort.

He took his first sip of coffee and settled in to read the article in its entirety. This was the first news of Freddie since he 'walked' on the assault charge. He'd heard nothing from him, and frankly, had no desire to.

As he neared the end of the article, he saw that the first Court appearance for the accused was scheduled for today. He could feel a rush of anxiety come over him as he almost ran to the front desk to get his phone messages from yesterday. He wasn't sure whether he should be disappointed or relieved to see the message from Freddie. He knew eventually he'd have to take care of this matter, however painful it might become.

It was easy for him to envision the awkwardness of this representation. Would it be all the more awkward should he not take the case? It was impossible to know for sure what Freddie might say. Scenarios were tumbling through his mind when the buzz of the intercom brought him back to the present.

"Yes?" he answered.

"Good morning," Elsie stated. "It's almost time for Court."

"Thank you, I'll be right out," Reddick replied as he folded up the paper and quickly put his folder of documents in his briefcase. He still had no idea what he would do when he confronted Freddie about the representation... guess he would have to cross that bridge when he came to it.

Reddick's business at the Courthouse was quickly completed. He decided he would wait around until Freddie's case was called and make the representation decision then. After about an hour, a deputy escorted Freddie into the courtroom. Reddick saw him looking around the room and knew that he was the object of the search. When he stepped forward, Freddie halfway smiled and appeared to relax and resume his normally cool demeanor.

"Tried to call you, man," Freddie said in a whisper. "I was hoping you'd take care of this for me."

Reddick said nothing to him. He only answered the Judge when asked about his intent to represent. After the amount of bail was set way beyond what the Court knew Mr. Johnson could afford, Reddick turned to Freddie. "I'll come to the jail to meet with you about the charges later this afternoon." With that, he closed up his briefcase and left the courtroom.

He was anxious about the meeting, to say the very least. He could only imagine what might be going through Freddie's mind. The entire matter was equivalent to walking a high wire without a net - afraid that Freddie might try to blackmail him if he did refuse to represent him, and afraid of what he might say or do in open Court if he did.

Reddick decided to have lunch alone in his office. He needed the time to ponder this delicate situation. After all, there was no one he could discuss this with... no one knew he'd paid Freddie to scare the crap out of the now-deceased faggots. He didn't even know if Freddie was the one who killed them! If Freddie wasn't guilty of the murders, what was he going to do - ask for his two hundred dollars back?

He quickly decided it would be best for him not to bring up the past... if he didn't mention it maybe Freddie wouldn't either. He realized he might never know for sure if Freddie committed the murders. So much time had passed... would it really matter now? ... he thought to himself. When he first learned of the murders, Reddick remembered thinking if Freddie mentioned he had been given money to scare the victims, he would implicate himself in the crime. That would be much worse than if Freddie admitted to him he'd used the money to get "high" and never did the job he was paid for.

This was not good any way you looked at it, Reddick thought to himself as he picked up the wrappings left from his lunch. He wadded them up in a tight ball and aimed for the trashcan by the door. He missed, just as his office door slowly opened.

"Did Bruce speak to you before he left?" Elsie asked somewhat puzzled.

"No, I haven't talked to him all morning," Reddick replied. "I didn't even know if he'd made it in today."

"He came in about thirty minutes ago. Right after I took a "Special Delivery" envelope back to him, he flew out of here like his pants were on fire. Normally I wouldn't worry, but he has court in a few minutes."

Reddick suddenly had a feeling of déjà vu. "Special Delivery? Who was it from?" Reddick questioned.

"I don't remember noticing a return address, but it had 'Personal and Confidential' written on the front."

Reddick immediately had a negative gut-wrenching feeling about the situation. He went into Bruce's office to see if he could find any indication of where he'd gone in such a hurry. He saw nothing except the folder for his court case placed in the center of his desk. He picked up the folder and headed for the Courthouse.

As Reddick waited for the case to be called, he kept a lookout for Bruce. No one had seen him all day. After a forty-five minute wait, the case number was called and Reddick approached the bench on behalf of his brother and the Firm. Getting a continuance was the best he could do on such short notice.

Reddick left the Courthouse and went around to the jail. He asked one of the deputies to give a message to Frederick Johnson. He handed the jailer a note telling him his attorney would be in to talk to him tomorrow afternoon, instead of today. Reddick thought Freddie would be as relieved about the postponement as he was.

Now to find Bruce, Reddick thought.

Reddick got back to the office to find that Bruce had still not returned. He picked up the phone and immediately started making calls.

First he tried Bruce's house. He wasn't there, but Sandra told Reddick about the fight they had a few days back. She filled him in on the details and it only added more reason for concern.

"He'd been drinking since the weekend before our fight and I couldn't get him to stop," Sandra said. "Reddick, I think he's doing drugs, too. He goes into a rage when I try to talk to him. He's irrational and out of control... I don't want him around the kids like that," she said.

"I understand, Sandra," Reddick said. "Do you have any idea where he might be?"

"No, not unless he's with the woman that called for him the other night," Sandra replied.

"What would make you think something like that?" Reddick questioned.

"When I told her Bruce wasn't here and asked to take a message, she said, 'That's okay, I'll probably see him before you do!'" Sandra said with a voice full of emotion.

"Now Sandra, don't let something like that bother you," Reddick soothed. "It's probably a prankster, or somebody he's sent to prison. We always get things like that.... you know how this business is... don't worry."

Reddick promised Sandra he'd call when he found Bruce, though she made it clear she didn't want him back home or around the children until he was sober.

For some unknown reason, Reddick sensed an impending crisis; he felt inexplicably consumed by fear for the first time since childhood. He realized Bruce was already experiencing some sort of crisis, and if the "Special Delivery" *was* what he thought it might be, it would be enough to push him over the edge.

Reddick picked up the phone again and called the Chief. He explained the chain of events and asked if he would assist in the search for Bruce.

"You know I'll do everything I can to help," the Chief said.

The Chief put all his men on the alert to watch for Bruce. "Quietly pick him up if you see him. Understand, we don't want to arrest him... he's sick, we just want to get some help for him," the Chief explained. His men understood completely. Next, the Chief called an associate he had not spoken with in a couple of years.

After the normal pleasantries and the catching up, the Chief explained the reason for his call to the Vice Squad Officer. "Looks like our boy may be trying to cash in on those stolen photographs," the Chief said. "Do you have any information from that end?"

"Funny you should ask," the officer replied. "We got a domestic call just last week. Seems our boy lost it and got real ugly with the little wife in front of the child. His father-in-law had him picked up the next day and he spent a few days in our "Hilton Arms" before his mother bailed him out."

"Sounds like things aren't going so well for the lad. Just proves money can't always buy happiness," the Chief chuckled. "Our situation here is speculative at best. It'll probably be a day or two before I can ascertain whether we have sufficient evidence on this end to have you pick him up. I'll get back to you as soon as I can."

"It would be my pleasure to 'bust' this pretty boy for you - just tell me when," the Vice Officer replied.

The Chief thanked the officer and told him he would be in touch as soon as the evidence was actually in his hands.

The Chief knew with this turn of events, Franks not only wasn't welcome in his own home, but also had lost his job. No income - no place to go! He then called Ben.

"Remember the photo lab we found at Gillespie's house right after the murders?" he asked.

"Sure do," Ben replied. "What about it?"

"Later we got that report Mike Franks and a couple of his buddies had broken in and stolen the photographs."

"I remember," Ben replied. "Franks moved to Charlottesville."

"We have reason to believe he may be back in our jurisdiction and up to no good. Could you have a deputy drive out to his mother's house and check it out?" the Chief asked.

"Sure thing," Ben replied. "I'll give you a call when I know something."

"I'd appreciate it, Ben," the Chief said as he hung up the receiver.

Meanwhile, Reddick had called Jimmy at the Blackbird, in addition to everyone else he could think of... seems no one had seen Bruce. After several unsuccessful attempts, he thought maybe he'd have more luck just driving around; maybe he could spot Bruce's car somewhere. This wasn't a very big town, but looking for Bruce would be like trying to find a needle in a haystack.

Reddick didn't go back to the office, but he did go by the house to tell Penny what was happening. After getting a heavier coat, a sandwich and the thermos of coffee Penny had fixed for him, he was back on the road. He drove to Ashton thinking maybe Bruce had hit the clubs over there... he struck out, no one had seen him.

After an hour, the Chief called Reddick's office to see if he had found Bruce.

"Chief, Reddick hasn't come back yet," Elsie said. "I'll ask him to call you as soon as he does."

****

Hours had passed and Reddick was still running the roads trying to find Bruce. He had almost run out of places to look, and he had definitely run out of daylight. Just as he was about to throw in the towel, he happened to remember something from back in their childhood. Bruce's favorite place in the world to play was in the barn at the farm. He wondered if there was a chance he might have driven up there.

He quickly made a u-turn and headed out into the country. It was a good thirty-minute drive out to the farm.

His thoughts quickly turned to the road conditions up there... the ground was still saturated from so much snow over the winter. It had mostly melted away except for the extreme north side in the higher elevations; however, the lack of sunshine had left the roads in an extremely muddy state. He thought about the one lane pig-trail of a road he would have to deal with once he left the main highway and hoped he wouldn't get stuck. The nearest neighbor was at least a quarter mile back down the road.

He pulled up to the gate and got out of the car. He could see with the car headlights the chain was wrapped around the post, but the lock was not fastened to it. That was a good indication someone was there, or had been there recently. The neighbor down the road kept an eye on the place. For years the Old Man had been trading him the use of a small pasture for the favor.

Reddick unwrapped the chain from the gate and opened it wide. He got back into the car and slowly pulled through the opening and continued on the winding road toward the old house and barn.

He was almost past the turn-off on the narrow lane that led down to the barn when he caught a glimpse of a small light. He backed up and turned toward the barn. As he got nearer, he could see there was a light coming from inside. He hurriedly pulled up in front of the barn doors and quietly got out of the car. He could clearly hear the engine of an automobile running. As he opened the door to the barn, he saw Bruce's car, lights on, engine running and Bruce slumped over his briefcase in the front seat. Reddick opened the driver door and immediately smelled the strong aroma of alcohol. When he looked down, there in the corner of the briefcase, he saw a bottle of prescription drugs.

Reddick panicked, "Bruce, Bruce wake up!" he yelled. There was no response. He tried to shake him awake, but still got nothing. Though his body temperature was low, Reddick managed to find a faint pulse.

He had to act quickly. There was no one around to help, so the only thing to do was to transfer him over into his car and get him back to town as soon as possible.

Reddick quickly put the empty pill bottle in his coat pocket and manhandled Bruce into the front seat of his Mercedes. He quickly went back inside the barn and turned off the lights and engine of Bruce's car. He grabbed the briefcase from the front seat and closed the barn door on his way out. Reddick hurriedly made his way back down the muddy road, leaving the gate open, knowing Mr. Metcalf would find it in the morning.

As soon as Reddick reached the highway, he opened up the Mercedes. Since buying it a few years back, there had never been any reason to see what she could do, but he certainly blew it out getting back to town. Once there, he didn't slow down one bit... he turned onto Fleming and was pulling up to emergency admitting in record time.

Bruce had not moved... it was difficult to know if he was even breathing. His vital signs were so weak Reddick wasn't sure he was even alive. Reddick bolted out of the car and opened the emergency room door yelling for help! A gurney was immediately rolled out to the car and Bruce was quickly wheeled in.

After giving the admitting room nurse the necessary information, Reddick went back out to move his car from the front door. As he pulled around into a more permanent parking space and turned off the engine, he glanced into the back seat at the briefcase. He pulled it into the seat beside him and opened it. There on top was an envelope marked "Special Delivery." He hesitated... he had never actually seen the pictures Bruce had told him about a few years ago when this mess blew up in their faces. He wondered if he had the courage to see them now, if in fact, that *was* what the envelope contained.

He had to know.... if this was the reason his brother had tried to kill himself, he just had to look. Slowly he opened the envelope. Sure enough, it contained more than a half-dozen glossy prints. He turned on the interior light of the car so he could actually see the content of the photographs. Reddick was shocked and embarrassed to see the explicit and provocative sex pictures. As he flipped through them, he better understood why Bruce was so upset. He couldn't imagine his brother participating in the activities indicated by them. There was absolutely no doubt it was Bruce; these photographs were unquestionably damning.

Reddick quickly returned the photos to the envelope and put it back inside the briefcase. He now realized he had a lot of calls to make.

****

Within the hour, a few close friends and relatives had gathered at the hospital. Recognizing the prominent status of their new patient, the hospital staff had kindly provided a private waiting room for the small group.

After what seemed like hours, the doctor appeared and called Reddick out into the hall. Dr. Slagle had been the family physician and close family friend for as long as he could remember. Reddick could tell by the doctor's demeanor the news was not good.

"How is he?" Reddick hesitantly asked.

The doctor looked at Reddick with a very solemn expression. "He *is* alive, only by the grace of God. I wish I could tell you the prognosis was good, but I'd be lying to you, Reddick. If he makes it through the night, I'll be surprised," the doctor sadly stated. "His body has already begun to shut down and he's in a coma. It's just too early to tell if he'll survive," he stated.

Dr. Slagle then placed his hand on Reddick's shoulder. "You'll have to tell Sandra, and I urge you to prepare your father for the worst. I'll call you if there's any change."

Reddick thanked the doctor as he turned to go back into the waiting room and face the group.

To those anxiously waiting, he emotionally relayed what the doctor had said. "Dr. Slagle indicated there wasn't any way to tell how long Bruce might be in this coma, *or* even if he would survive. There's no use waiting here," he said. "Dr. Slagle said he'd call if there's any change."

It took a few minutes for the reality of the news to sink in. Penny suggested that someone should stay... to be there in case Bruce regained consciousness. After a short discussion, they collectively concluded that some- one would need to be rested to sit tomorrow in case his condition had not changed. Penny announced she would stay the night. Everyone else in the group decided to go home to wait for news on Bruce's condition.

"I guess I'd better go over and tell Sandra what's hap- pened. I'll be back as soon as I can," he said as he kissed Penny on the cheek. "I'll break the news to Mom and Dad first thing in the morning," he added.

Reddick was not anxious to confront Sandra at this hour, but he recognized his obligation. As he drove the short distance to the house, he mentally rehearsed what he planned to say. He had no intentions of telling her the whole story... he didn't feel the need to drudge up the painful past.

Soon he was on the front porch ringing the bell. The porch light came on in a few minutes and Sandra expectantly opened the door.

****

The Chief had arrived and was waiting with Penny when Reddick got back to the hospital. He had gotten Reddick's call earlier and decided to come up to lend his support for the family.

Penny had already passed along the medical information from Dr. Slagle, but the Chief had yet to be informed of all the details.

Almost immediately the two friends excused themselves to find a cup of coffee. In addition to finding the coffee, they wanted to find a place to discuss this sensitive situation without being overheard. Reddick filled the Chief in on how he found Bruce and he had, in fact, found the pictures in the car. "The postmark on the envelope was from Charlottesville, Chief," Reddick stated. "There was a detailed demand note this time... I don't think there will be any trouble in matching the handwriting. Franks even gave a drop location for the extortion money."

"Son-of-a-bitch!" the Chief exclaimed. "I don't see how he can wiggle out of this!" The Chief then went on to explain he had called the Vice Officer in Charlottesville to alert him to the potential situation. "He said he would be happy to pick him up... we just needed to let him know when and what the charges would be," the Chief said as he sipped his hot coffee.

"How much of this does your Dad know?" the Chief then asked.

"None, yet," Reddick replied. "I planned to go over in the morning and break the bad news about Bruce. I don't want to burden them with anything else. At this point, it wouldn't serve any purpose... it'll be plenty hard on them as it is."

The two finished up their coffee and Reddick prepared two cups to go. It was going to be a very long night.

****

Reddick and Penny had waited through the night with no further word from the doctor or nurses about Bruce's condition. They had tried to get comfortable enough to doze, but really got little rest.

First thing the following morning, Sandra came in. Judging from the way she was dressed and the baggage she was carrying, it appeared she had planned to stay for the day. "Any news?" she asked as she patted Reddick on the shoulder and stooped to hug Penny.

"Nothing since last night," Penny replied.

Just as Sandra was putting down her bags and preparing to sit down, Dr. Slagle entered the room.

Reddick stood to greet him and shake his hand. "Any change?" he asked.

"Well, we *have* been able to stabilize him, but he's still in a coma. I wish I had better news, but there's no way of knowing how long he could be this way."

"Is there anything more we could do... do you have any suggestions?" Reddick questioned.

"Well, we can continue to watch him for a day or so, then if there's no significant change, we could transfer him down to Duke to be evaluated. They're better equipped for this type of thing... they can run tests and get information we'd never be able to get here."

"Whatever you think is best, of course, is exactly what we want to do," Reddick stated as he looked over at Sandra.

Sandra knew Reddick would be making the family decisions now that the Old Man was not well. It didn't matter that it should have been her decision; she was in total agreement with it. "Yes, yes, you're right, whatever is best for Bruce," she agreed, grateful Reddick had taken the initiative to speak up first. He was relieved she was so quick to agree with him. They both knew Bruce would be receiving the best care money could buy.

It was at that moment he acknowledged a strange feeling of responsibility... it was then he realized *"the scepter of family rule had been successfully passed."*

After the doctor had given his report and left the small waiting room, the three discussed the need for someone to be there until Bruce's condition changed or Dr. Slagle transferred him down state. Sandra said she was prepared to stay until late afternoon, at which time she would need to pick up the children from her Mother's house. Penny would go home, get some sleep and return later in the afternoon about the time Sandra would have to leave. They agreed this arrangement would work for a day or two. Someone needed to be there in case there was a change in Bruce's condition, or hopefully he regained consciousness.

Reddick was apprehensive, but knew his obligation to tell his Mom and Dad what had happened to Bruce. For years they had been aware of some of the demons that haunted their younger son, but they had no need to know about all of them.

As he drove down the street leading to his parents' house, he entertained memories of childhood. He and Bruce must have climbed every tree on the street at one time or the other and he was sure they had been chased out of more than one backyard garden. They slept in their imaginary fort in the backyard for at least a week before the rain chased them back inside to their room. He smiled as he fought back the tears his manhood refused to accept.

"Mom?" he called out as he let himself in the kitchen door.

"In here," he heard her reply. "Reddick, I'm surprised to see you today, son. Is everything alright?" she asked, knowing very well something was wrong.

"Mom, where's Dad?" Reddick asked as he went into the laundry room where his mother was ironing a shirt.

"He's sitting out in the Florida room enjoying the sunshine," she replied. "Why, is something wrong?"

"Mom, can you come out with me, I have something to tell you and Dad," he said, trying to stay as calm as possible.

Mrs. Munroe turned off the iron and walked out to the Florida room and sat down across from her childhood sweetheart, the man she had loved for forty-five years.

His father looked up at him with a puzzled expression and asked why he wasn't at the office. Reddick knew his father's "good" day was just about to end.

As calmly as possible he described the events leading up to the visit. He deliberately omitted the facts that would have completely devastated them. Initially, his mother was visibly upset, but soon was resigned to the fact that everything possible was being done. His father just sat in his chair without expression, adjusting and readjusting the small blanket that had been placed over his legs. He asked Reddick a few pertinent questions, verifying he had heard and understood everything he had been told.

After answering all the questions his parents had asked and reassuring them as best he could, Reddick told them he needed to go. He explained he had to check by the office and then return to the hospital. He promised he would call them later in the day after the doctor made his afternoon rounds.

As Reddick drove back to the office, he felt a sense of relief. He thought both his parents had taken the news very well, under the circumstances. Mom was always more emotional than Dad had ever been... he had always been harder to read, calm and calculating; rarely letting his emotions get the best of him.

Having accomplished the most difficult task of the day, he swung by the office to bring Elsie up-to-speed. She was busy at her desk and didn't immediately look up. As Reddick reached for his messages, the motion of his hand startled her.

"Where have you been?" she quipped. "Am I supposed to run this office all by myself?" she asked with a taunting smile.

Reddick failed to see her humor this morning. "Can you come back for a minute?" he asked, motioning toward his office.

The smile faded from her face as she rose from her chair and headed down the hall behind him.

"What is it, Reddick?" she asked as she followed him into what was once his father's office.

"Sit down for a minute. I need to tell you something important," he started.

For the second time that day he relayed the same bad news. When he got to the part about finding Bruce in the barn, tears started to stream down the face of his motherly secretary. Reddick knew Elsie cared more for the two of them than she would ever admit. After all, they had grown up under her feet... how could she not love them? Just as he had told his mother, "Everything possible is being done at this point. Dr. Slagle will do everything in his power and use every means at his disposal to help Bruce. All we can do is to pray for a miracle."

"I know I have an appointment to see Frederick Johnson this afternoon," Reddick continued. "Could you call over to the jail and set it up for eleven this morning? Then clear my calendar for a few days. Oh, and while you're at it, reschedule Bruce's appointments around mine. I know it won't be easy, but do the best you can."

"Anything else I can do?" she asked as she soberly left the chair and started out the door.

"I guess not - nothing I can think of," he sincerely answered. The long hours and stress were beginning to take their toll. Suddenly he felt exhausted.

He reached for the paperwork on the Johnson case. He knew he should be apprehensive and very anxious about seeing Johnson, but he was just too tired. He looked over the charges and checked a few references related to the charge of forgery. By the time he had made a few notes, it was almost eleven.

He grabbed his coat and briefcase and made his way down the hall.

"You look rough," Elsie said.

"Yeah, I know a shave and a clean shirt would help, but there's no time right now," he replied as he continued out the front door.

He walked the few blocks to the jail. The overcast skies and the brisk wind whipped through the streets, sending a chill to the bone. He turned down by the Courthouse... the jail was situated on the backside of the block. When he walked in, two or three deputies whom he had known for the most of his life greeted him.

"Got Johnson in the interview room, boys?" Reddick asked as he walked past the group.

"He's ready for you, Reddick," they replied almost in unison.

Reddick walked down the hall past the elevator to the first door on the right. He peered through the glass to see Freddie sitting at the table inside. He could see his hands in the middle of the table with his wrists in cuffs. He slowly opened the door. As he entered the room, the attending deputy rose to leave. "I'll be just outside the door if you need me," he said as he excused himself.

Reddick placed his briefcase on the table and opened it as he sat down.

Freddie's eyes followed every move. "Been a long time," he spoke as he looked for a reaction from Reddick.

"Yes, I guess it has."

"Look, Mr. Munroe," Freddie started. "I just want you to know - I didn't kill those guys. Murphy and I went over there to see 'em that Sunday, just like you said... but we couldn't find 'em anywhere. We ran into a guy that had some goof balls, and you know, one thing just led to another. I was gonna' take care of that for you, but I guess somebody got to 'em before I did."

"I didn't come here to talk about that, Freddie," Reddick firmly stated. The tone of his voice left no mistake that he didn't want to discuss the subject further. "Tell me about this forgery charge."

Their eyes met across the interview table. Without a word, there was an unmistakable understanding. From that point on, the subject of the murders was never to be brought up again by either of the men.

When the interview was finished, Reddick walked back to the office. Rightfully, he should have been relieved, but he was just too drained to give it any thought.

****

He grabbed his messages as he made his way back to his office. He planned to return the calls that simply couldn't wait, go home and shower, and then go back to the hospital.

He was working his way through the stack of messages and had completed a couple of the calls when Elsie appeared at his office doorway with tears streaming down her face. "Your Mother just called to say that your father has taken a turn for the worse... *she wants you to come... now*!"

Reddick dropped the phone receiver and reached for his jacket. He was out the door, leaving Elsie standing in the middle of his office. As she walked to his desk to replace the phone receiver, she sadly looked around the room as years of fond memories flashed through her mind. She turned off the light as she walked out, gently pulling the door closed behind her.

****

For the first time in days, Reddick was finally alone. It seemed years ago since he had gotten the call about his Dad. The Old Man had passed very quickly. Reddick suspected that it was the news about Bruce that had caused it... probably he would never know for sure.

He went to the only place he knew he could find solitude, the Beacon Club. He sat quietly at the small table in the kitchen gazing into his almost empty glass. He had just come from the cemetery and was still dressed in the dark gray suit he had worn to his father's funeral. As he fixed another drink, he felt a surge of pride that his father was so very well liked and respected. The mourners had filled the funeral parlor to overflowing and the procession to the cemetery had literally stretched for blocks and blocks.

Though he felt completely lost, at least here, he could let his emotional guard down. Dealing with the events of the past week had rendered him mentally and physically exhausted. He had endured what he thought to be the worst nightmare he could recall in all of his forty-some years.

The loss of his father had been a great blow; regardless of how prepared he thought he might have been. The reality of 'the possibility of death' never really sinks in until it actually occurs. Reddick wondered if he would ever be able to fill the shoes his father had worn for so very long.

Who would have ever thought that in the matter of a week, life could become so twisted? Reddick felt some unknown force had consumed his world... it had taken away those he loved and for some unknown reason, had spit him out alone... it had rejected him.

Bruce had been taken to Duke for testing; however, the doctor informed the family that without significant improvement he might need to remain there. Although he was still clinging to life, he possibly could remain in a coma indefinitely... Dr. Slagle hadn't given much hope for recovery.

Just as Reddick got up to mix himself another drink, he glanced out the window to see the Chief pulling into the drive. He instinctively got another glass and mixed one for the Chief as well. A few minutes later, the door opened and the Chief came in carrying a large file box, which he placed in the center of the table.

"What's this?" Reddick asked as he sat the two glasses down.

"Neilson sent us a gift," the Chief replied.

"Who's Neilson?" Reddick asked as he removed the lid of the box. "Holy Shit!" he immediately exclaimed as he looked down into the box. It must have contained *hundreds* of negatives and prints.

"Seems a few weeks ago, Franks' wife found the naughty photographs," the Chief started. "As you can imagine, they had a big fight and her father had him picked up. She said she had hidden the pictures after their fight... then last night, Franks went back to get 'em. *All hell* broke loose. Neilson said a call came in about 2:30 this morning. Franks showed up at the house demanding the pictures, she refused and he got a little rough. When Neilson and a couple of other officers got to the scene, Franks was armed and threatening to kill her. Neilson said he had no choice but to shoot Franks in self defense."

"And this?" Reddick questioned as he placed his hands on either side of the box.

"She handed them over to Neilson... said to get them out of her house," the Chief answered. "They won't need 'em as evidence since they have nothing to do with the domestic case. She had a protective order against him and they have the gun he was waving around. It was a clear-cut case of *Assault with Intent*."

Reddick slowly lowered himself back into his chair, somewhat dazed from the impact of their new acquisition. After so many years of anxiety over the murders, the blackmail and the rumors, *some sort of resolution...*

an end to this hellish nightmare... now seemed to be a reality...

"It's over, Chief, by God - it's finally over!"
      .... if somehow Bruce could only know.

Acknowledgments ....

I owe a special debt of gratitude to Bill, my source of inspiration, for his hours of patience and many miles of travel relative to the making of this book. I am very grateful to Sondra for sharing her ideas for the characters in the storyline. I would especially like to thank my dear friend Lois, who repeatedly traveled so far to encourage and assist me with the story. I also want to thank my friend and editing assistant, Susan, for her infinite patience and sharp editing skills. I wish to extend my appreciation to Edgar Schoen for sharing his insight and knowledge of the publishing business and finally my thanks to John for his help and computer wizardry.

Last but not least, my heart-felt thanks goes to those special few, who wish to remain anonymous for their information, guidance and valued words of encouragement.

Printed in the United States
216788BV00002B/2/P